MW01134199

Boystown 7

Bloodlines

Marshall Thornton

Los Angeles
2015

Copyright © 2015 Marshall Thornton

This book is a work of fiction. Names, characters, places, and incidents are products of the author's imagination or are used fictitiously. Any resemblance to actual events or locales or persons, living or dead, is entirely coincidental.

This book is licensed to the original purchaser only. Duplication or distribution via any means is illegal and a violation of International Copyright Law, subject to criminal prosecution and upon conviction, fines and/or imprisonment.

All rights reserved, including the right of reproduction in whole or in part in any form.

Published by Kenmore Books
Edited by Joan Martinelli
Cover design by Marshall Thornton
Image by lanak via 123rf

ISBN-13: 978-150854712
ISBN-10: 150854715

First Edition

I would like to thank my readers, editors, and memory checkers: Danielle Wolff, Joan Martinelli, Helene Augustyniak, Peter Garino, Miles Ketchum, Vincent Diamond and Ellen Sue Feinberg. I'd particularly like to thank Lemise Rory for her sage legal advice.

Chapter One

Tax day fell on a Monday that year, the sixteenth. The sky was full of gray clouds and peoples' moods were just as colorless. For a change, it wasn't a bad day for me. In fact, I was in something resembling a good mood. I'd spent most of the year before bartending and having taxes withheld so I didn't have to struggle through the normally complicated question of whether I'd made a profit from my private investigation business. In fact, I was expecting a small tax refund. Money in the mail was always worth being happy about. But more than that, I was working again, and while that would complicate my 1984 taxes, I was making good money and it was more interesting than pouring flat beer and sour wine.

Around two o'clock, there was a knock on my office door and, before I could yell "Come in," Owen Lovejoy, Esquire whooshed in. He was a friend, a fuck buddy, occasionally my attorney, and, at that particular moment, my boss. I tended to think of him as Owen Lovejoy, Esquire because that's the way he first introduced himself. A good-looking guy, he's on the taller side of short, thick-bodied and brown-haired. He favors tortoise-shell glasses with lenses that cover most of his face, and well-tailored suits that cost twice what I make in a good week. He sat down on the two cardboard boxes full of paperwork that I'd stacked in front of my desk as a temporary guest chair.

"I have a job I need you to do," he said.

That confused me. I was already doing a job for him. Quite a complicated job, in fact. I began to reply but all I got out was the word, "But—" before he raised his hand to silence me. I stared at him, trying to think the situation through.

Late in February of that year I'd begun working for Cooke, Babcock and Lackerby. Every week I sent them an invoice for seven hundred dollars. Under services rendered I typed RETAINER. At Owen's request, I never sent an itemized bill. I also never sent a single report describing what I'd found. My reports were given verbally on windy street corners, busy diners, even once in bed. After Owen and I fucked, he'd turned the radio on loud and I whispered what I'd learned. The case was important. It had to do with Jimmy English.

A menagerie of Federal, State and City agencies had formed a task force and were months or maybe even weeks away from indicting Jimmy on a host of charges. At the top of the stack were a couple of murders. Owen assured me that Jimmy hadn't had anything to do with the murders under investigation, while at the same time never claiming that Jimmy hadn't been involved in at least a couple other murders along the way. I knew Jimmy, had done a little work for him, and probably owed my current position to his good graces. If Jimmy said he didn't kill someone he probably didn't. More importantly, he was too smart a guy to waste time lying to his own attorney.

Now, why the task force wanted to get him for two murders he didn't commit was something of a question. They either mistakenly believed he'd been involved in the murders, or, knowing he been involved in other murders, decided it didn't matter much what murder they nabbed him for as long as he went to prison. My job was to learn everything the task force had. That might sound challenging, but as it turned out it wasn't especially hard.

On the second day of my employment with Cooke, Babcock and Lackerby, Owen had shown up at my office with a moving man. My office is above a copy place on Clark and on that particular February morning it was what I'd politely call a mess. Much of the furniture from my abandoned apartment was still being stored there. I'd gotten rid of a few things; the bed for instance, which in my last days with Harker had developed a dip in the middle. The dip was fine if I planned to be constantly sliding into it to meet someone I loved, but sooner or later I'd be living on my own again and I couldn't face sliding into the dip alone. So I'd let it go.

The moving guy brought fifteen cardboard boxes into my office in two trips. He was heavily-muscled, tall, just a little over thirty, and had barely broken a sweat bouncing all those boxes around. I had a sneaking suspicion that Owen would try to seduce him the minute they were done with me. That thought created some pretty pictures in my head, so I wasn't paying a lot of attention when Owen asked the moving guy to step out into the hall.

"Was he bad? Are you punishing him?"

"Sweetheart, you need to remember something very important." He leaned in and spoke very clearly, "We were never here."

4 | Marshall Thornton

"Okay."

"And if anyone ever asks, you did not get these boxes from us."

"Where did I get them?"

"Yard sale? No, I'm joking. You don't need to worry your pretty head about that. If push comes to shove, we'll make sure you're never asked."

"What's in them?"

"Everything the task force has on Jimmy English."

"How did you get all this?"

He smiled. "I didn't get it. I was never here. Remember?"

"What am I supposed to do with these boxes that fell out of the sky?"

"For now? Read everything. Learn everything. Know it all backwards and forwards."

I nodded. Eventually, if there were a trial, all of this information would come to the defense as part of discovery. Well, most of it anyway. I was going to be responsible for making sure nothing got conveniently dropped by the government. Particularly if that something was favorable to Jimmy. Of course, I also saw exactly why Cooke, Babcock and Lackerby didn't want to be connected to the materials until they received them directly from the State's Attorney's office. At that moment, there was no indictment, so it wasn't exactly legal for anyone to have them. Dropping the files on me allowed them to have them and not have them.

"This is the last time we can talk in your office. We'll make other arrangements."

"You think my office is bugged?"

"Not yet, dear. This is your second day. It will be by the end of the week, though."

"If I'm working for you then they can't bug my office. Doesn't privilege extend—"

"Privilege depends on the situation, on the judge who's ruling, on which way the wind is blowing off Lake Michigan. Look, if I explain anymore than that we'll both fall asleep. Trust me, your office will be bugged. And soon."

"Can you fight it? Go to the judge—"

"There is no judge. It's not legal surveillance."

In Chicago legal niceties were sometimes skipped. They couldn't present an illegal wiretap in court but they could act on information they gleaned by creating other routes to discover whatever they'd learned. Treasure hunts are always easier if you already know where the treasure is.

Still, my sense of justice was a tad outraged. "Let's catch them at it. Let's take them down."

"They've been caught before. Had their hands slapped. The only lesson they learned was to be more careful. There will be several impenetrable layers between the task force and the bug. Anything they hear that they want to use, they'll feed to an informant."

"They can't create their own testimony."

"Darling you watch too much TV. The law is not about right and wrong. It's about what you can get away with on a given day."

After he left, I got down to business with the boxes and almost immediately started having a good time. They were full of interviews, witness statements, crime reports, depositions, transcripts from wiretaps (legal ones), and transcripts from a few peripherally related trials. Over the next few weeks I'd mentally cross-referenced everything. I knew where it all was and I knew what it all meant. I had two very important things I needed to discuss with Owen, so I wasn't especially happy that he was trying to give me another job.

"All right. Tell me about this job," I said.

"I'm sure you've heard of Madeline Levine-Berkson?"

"Yes and no," I said. Madeline Levine-Berkson was a dentist whose husband, Wes Berkson, made the mistake of telling her about an affair he was having while she was making dinner. Dr. Levine-Berkson stopped chopping vegetables and stuck the rather large knife she'd been using into her husband's chest. At first the case garnered a lot of press, and it was obvious the reporters were dying to get their hands on the mistress; an interview with her would have sold papers hand over greedy fist. But, they couldn't find her. And, worse, Dr. Levine-Berkson refused to claim any justification other than the unproven infidelity, so the case was quietly relegated to the back section of most papers.

"Wasn't she convicted?" I asked.

"Yes. But it was still a victory."

"It was?"

"They charged her with first-degree murder and second-degree murder. The jury got to choose which they thought she was guilty of. They went with second degree."

"Okay, I still don't know what you want me to do."

"We have a two-week continuance to prepare for sentencing. The minimum the jury is allowed to impose is four years probation. That's our best hope. Worst case scenario she'll be sentenced to twenty years. If it's twenty years she'll serve ten or twelve, possibly more. She'll be lucky to get out in time to see her children graduate high school. Not to mention she'll be a confirmed lesbo by then."

That jogged my memory. The high school part, not the lesbo part. There were two small children involved, which could work in her favor. Children *do* need their mothers. Though, when you kill a child's father you're unlikely to win an award for good parenting.

"How many women on the jury? That should work in her favor."

Most women would not stab a cheating spouse; most did understand the impulse.

"Seven," Owen said. But then a cloud passed over his face. "The state made a big to-do about an insurance policy during the trial. Trying to make a case for first degree. I'm not sure one or two didn't believe that."

"Refresh my memory. What was their case?"

"The Berksons had taken out million dollar policies on each other."

"She was a dentist and he was…"

"Frequently unemployed."

"But she admits stabbing him so she'll never collect. How could that be first degree?"

"The ASA tried to make it sound like she didn't understand the fine print."

"She's smart enough to plot a murder but too stupid to understand an insurance policy?"

"He spent a lot of time reading the policy into the record. Claimed even he had trouble understanding it."

"She's a dentist. She has an education."

"She went to dental school in the Caribbean. Wasn't at the top of her class."

"Still. No offense, but I think law school is a lot easier." Science had never been a strong suit of mine.

Owen shrugged. "I thought it was crap, too. I'm absolutely certain she did not kill her husband for any insurance money she thought she'd get. She's very bright, and quite nice for a murderess. Fortunately, the jury agreed and threw out the first-degree charges."

"So what do you want me to do? Find the mistress?"

"I can't ask you to do that."

"I work for you, you can ask—"

"Madeline doesn't want her found. We do have to respect the client's wishes."

That struck me as odd. The mistress would have bolstered her story and created sympathy.

"Is there even a mistress?" I wondered.

"The newspapers tried awfully hard to find her," he said absently. "But then...journalists, they don't always have the right skills."

He wanted me to find the mistress. I hadn't spent much time working for him, but I had the feeling we'd be having a lot of conversations that were not directly about what they were about.

"Isn't it kind of pointless to find her now? Your client still won't appreciate it."

"No, she won't. But…" I could see the wheels turning. "If someone found her by *accident* it could be helpful."

"If she exists."

"Yes, if she exists. I wouldn't want her in court but…*someone* could get her interviewed by the *Daily Herald* or *The Tribune*."

"How would that help?"

"The jury. They're not supposed to read the newspaper during the trial. Most of them take that very seriously. But she's been convicted. At least a couple of them will have jumped the gun and be back to reading the newspaper or watching the nightly news. Not to mention discussing it with their families. If the woman were to do an interview, the jury would know it."

"So I need to accidentally find her."

Owen's lips were sealed. In fact, he kept them tightly closed. Instead, he picked up his briefcase, chocolate brown leather with his initials engraved in gold leaf. O.W.L. I wondered what the "W" was for. Or even if it was *for* anything. It might just be that he liked to think of himself as an owl. Owls were wise. He pulled out a sheet of paper and slid it onto my desk. On it was a column of names; six of the names were typewritten, seven were added by hand.

"The names on the top are the witnesses who've agreed to testify on Madeline's behalf. The names on the bottom are those who've refused. Start with the ones who've refused. If nothing else, try to get them to come in and speak on Madeline's behalf. A couple of them might really help her."

The list didn't mean much at the moment. I decided to figure it out later. I really needed to talk to him about Jimmy English. "Um, why don't I walk you out?"

"Yes, why don't you."

I really didn't think my office was bugged. I'd been sticking the cover from a matchbook in between the door and the jamb just below the hinge whenever I left the office. If someone picked the lock and entered my office the little square of cardboard would have fallen to the floor. So far, it had stayed just where I'd left it.

Silently, we walked out of my office and down the narrow stairs to Clark Street. As soon as we were out the door, I said, "Look, I've got to tell—" He raised his hand to silence me again. It all seemed a bit ridiculous. He stepped out into the street and hailed a cab. We climbed in, and before giving the driver an address Owen took a twenty out of his pocket and waved it in the front seat. "We're just going around the block a few times. So, the rest is for you." He dropped the twenty on the seat and then closed the plexiglass partition between us.

Turning to me, he said, "All right, what's the problem?"

"I've figured out a couple of things about Operation Tea and Crumpets." Operation Tea and Crumpets was the cutesy name the task force had given the investigation into Jimmy's activities. "I'm not sure it's a good idea for me to step away right now."

"Then don't. Do both." I started to say that I wasn't sure it would be fair to either client but he stopped me by adding, "Keep billing us the retainer for Jimmy. And also whatever work you do for the Levine case." What that meant was that my invoicing could easily go over a thousand dollars a week. For about two weeks. That made the whole thing more appealing. I might need to work night and day, but it was just for a while. Part of me still wanted to say no to the lady dentist, but I was fresh out of good reasons.

"What did you find out on Jimmy?" Owen asked.

"The most damaging information comes from a single source. A confidential informant they call Prince Charles. There's no information in the files about who Prince Charles is. Not even a hint. Which makes me think that they know you have the files. That they wanted you to have them."

"They'll have to expose him eventually."

"So why go to the trouble of hiding him unless they know we're likely to get our hands on the files now?"

"You think it's a haystack with no needle."

"It might be. According to the transcripts, Jimmy told Prince Charles stories. Almost as though he was bragging, which seems out of character."

"I agree."

"And there's another thing. There's a book or a diary somewhere."

"Somewhere? But it's not in the boxes I gave you?"

"No. But a lot of the files have notations. Page numbers and dates."

"Something like that would be a terrific piece of evidence. Especially if it corroborates Prince Charles' testimony."

"But Jimmy's too smart for all of this." I resisted the temptation to say, "Something's fishy."

"I hope so," Owen said before he told the cab driver to pull over. We were at the corner of Belmont and Clark for the second time. Just as he got out the door, Owen said, "We need to know who's talking. And we need that book."

It was a tall order. A very tall order.

Chapter Two

Having sex with friends seems like a very good idea until suddenly it doesn't.

I'd moved in with my friend Brian Peerson after I'd been stabbed by a murderous young secretary. Fortunately, the girl's weapon of choice was poison; her skills with a letter opener were not as impressive. Most nights I slept in Brian's bed because his second bedroom was occupied by a sixteen year-old named Terry Winkler who'd been kicked out by his parents. The sex we had was good, fun, different even. I wanted to call him a fuck buddy, which he was— but he wasn't. And that made things different in bed. A good fuck buddy is someone who's friendly and likes sex and doesn't want to fall in love with you. Brian was all of those things. But he also cared about me and I cared about him. I cared about Ross, whom he loved, and I think he cared about Harker, whom I loved. That made sex between us different. Better. And worse. Occasionally, when I felt like things between Brian and I were getting too comfortable, I slept on the settee in the living room, which was anything but comfortable. I knew I needed to find myself an apartment, but I kept not doing anything about it.

When I got home that evening, I found Terry playing Atari in the living room and a note from Brian on his bed asking me to sleep on the settee that night. Since he wasn't there, I couldn't ask him what that was about. He'd never asked me to sleep in the living room before. In fact, he'd always seemed a little wounded when I chose to.

I wandered back into the living room and asked Terry, "Where's Brian?"

"Huh?" he asked, too into his game to hear me.

"Where's Brian?" A little louder this time.

"He went somewhere."

"He say where?"

Terry shook his head, but didn't take his attention off the television.

"So you have no idea? None?"

"He was wearing a really tight T-shirt and a lot of cologne." He threw a shrug in, as though what he said might not mean what it obviously meant. Brian was on his way out to meet someone. It might be someone he'd already met or it might be someone he hadn't yet met, but either way he intended to bring him home.

Part of me felt that it was wrong. He and Ross had broken up six or eight months before, when Ross moved downstate in hopes of a miracle cure. I suppose it was enough time for Brian to be thinking about moving on. Certainly, he'd been messing around with me for the last few months, but that wasn't moving on. Sex with me wasn't going anywhere. The idea of him getting over Ross enough to see someone new, well, I wasn't as comfortable with that as I should have been. I couldn't spend too much time thinking about it, though. I had two cases to work and needed to get busy.

I walked through the apartment to the back door. Sitting there was a stack of newspapers. Brian was careful to ask if I was finished with them before they went downstairs to the garbage. Each time he asked I hemmed and hawed, mostly because I felt more comfortable with at least two to three weeks of papers sitting around. I'd brought home the list of names Owen had given me and before I talked to them I needed to understand who these people were. The newspapers would help with that.

Bringing them out to the dining room, I sat down and began to dig through for stories about Madeline Levine-Berkson. There were seven people who'd refused to testify and six who'd agreed. I needed to see if any of the names appeared in the stories. That would tell me how they related to Madeline. Working backward, I found the most recent story on the trial was just the day before—Sunday. The article recapped everything right up to the defense resting that previous Friday; as luck would have it, Friday the Thirteenth. Closing statements were made; the jury went out to deliberate. Two hours later the jury was back and Madeline Levine was convicted of second-degree murder. By the end of the trial the papers had dropped the Berkson and just referred to her as Madeline Levine, as though by killing her husband she'd lost the right to use his name.

The article had several pictures. One was of a much younger Madeline Levine with her husband. She was a slightly pudgy bottle-blonde with naturally curly hair that formed a ball around her head. He was square-chinned handsome with a blurry look in his eyes. Another shot was of Madeline in court. She had a stern look on her face and her hair was pulled back, her curls forming a poodle ball over her forehead. It was dark now. I imagine they don't hand out hair dye in the women's section of the Cook County Jail.

In the wrap-up, I found several of the names I was looking for. Mrs. Jasper Levine of Park Ridge, Madeline's mother, had testified for the state about the poor quality of her daughter's marriage to Wes Berkson. She was one of those refusing to testify on her daughter's behalf. Insurance salesman Herb Dotson testified for the state that he sold the Berkson's insurance just a week before the murder. His name wasn't on either list. There was, however, a Nan Dotson on the "testify for" side of the list. It wasn't a likely coincidence she and the insurance agent had the same name. I guessed that they were married neighbors of Madeline's. I could be wrong, but until I found out differently that's what they were going to be. Dr. Caspian, the dentist who shared Madeline's practice, testified for the state. He was questioned extensively about Madeline's intelligence, her credentials as a dentist, and the quality of her Caribbean education. It wasn't particularly favorable testimony. He had refused to testify on Madeline's behalf, just as her mother had.

The defense took over and called a handful of witnesses. Melody Oddy, who turned out to be Madeline's sister, also testified about the crap relationship Madeline had with her husband. She, however, managed to imply that the problems in their relationship were mostly Wes's fault. She was "testify for." Lana Shepherd, a childhood friend of Madeline Levine, testified that Madeline had talked to her about Wes's suspicious behavior. Her testimony created a picture of a woman who suspected her husband might be cheating, who then went over the edge when she got confirmation. The Assistant State's Attorney pressed her on the issue of what Madeline knew for sure, attempting to get Lana to say that Madeline was certain of the affair prior to her husband's telling her—which would have made it first degree. Lana was scheduled to testify for Madeline. The last name I recognized was a woman named Lynn Hagen. She was the Berkson's babysitter. During the trial she claimed to have seen Wes Berkson with a woman she didn't know one weekend when Madeline was out of town at a dental convention. The ASA tried to cast doubt on whether or not Lynn told Madeline about the mysterious woman. She was on the "testify for" list.

I took a Marlboro out of the box, tapped it down, and lit it. I had some things to consider. Owen wanted me to start with the people who refused to testify on Madeline's behalf. I wondered if that was wise. In order to convince the seven people who'd refused to testify to change their minds, I had to understand what was going on with the case. I was more likely to get information I could use from the friendly witnesses.

Brian kept his telephone on a stand in the front room. In the bottom of the stand was a Chicago Greater Metropolitan Phonebook. I went into the living room, ignoring the beeps and bings and bangs coming from the TV, and looked up Melody Oddy. Of course, I expected to not find her number there. Her name was different from her family so her phone might be listed under a husband's name. Or if she was single it might not be listed at all. As I ran a finger down the O's I expected to find her in the 'burbs, if at all. I assumed she lived out near Park Ridge, like her parents. But there she was. On Wellington.

I dialed the number and after four rings a woman answered.

"Hi, is this Melody?"

"No. She's at work. Who's this?"

"This is Nick Nowak. I'm an investigator working on her sister's trial."

"Oh," the woman said with great disappointment. "Isn't that over?"

"Almost. Can you tell me where she works?"

"I don't know if that's a good idea. I don't know who you are." Then she asked, "Are you in an arcade or someplace?"

I could have asked Terry to turn down the TV or explained, but instead just said, "No. I'm not. Look, I can call back tomorrow, but things are little time sensitive. The sentencing is in two weeks."

"Well, you wouldn't have time to talk to her anyway. They just opened a few weeks ago."

"Who just opened?"

She hesitated. "I suppose it's okay. She works at a place called Crawdaddy. Seafood. You won't even be able to get in. It's that busy."

It was a Monday. I didn't think it could be that busy. Besides, I was beginning to get hungry. I thanked the girl, who I assumed was Melody's roommate, and hung up. I stood there thinking about what to do with Terry. He was sixteen so he didn't need a babysitter. But he also wasn't the kind of kid I liked leaving alone. His behavior for the last two months had been basically good, except for a couple of isolated incidents. One of which included his answering a personals ad from the back of the *Reader* resulting in a very unhappy twenty-six–year-old man showing up at Brian's door who nearly got a punch in the nose from me.

"Hey," I said, trying to get his attention. "Hey, Terry, listen up." Finally, he deigned to look at me. "I'm going out for dinner. You want to come?"

He said no in a way that managed to convey the sheer stupidity of my question.

"Is there something here for you to eat?" I asked.

"I dunno."

My first thought was that I should just leave and call him in an hour to see how he was doing. But that posed several problems. First, he might not answer the phone and then I'd be freaked out about whatever he was doing. Second, I knew there was food in the house, Brian wouldn't go out and let the kid starve. But the food was probably healthy which meant Terry might not want anything to do with it. He had a generous allowance so he could easily order in. Which led to the third problem. He was a good-looking boy, well, young man. In fact, at first glance he looked to be about twenty-two. He was well on his way to being as tall as I was, had dishwater blond hair, and his skin was clear and peachy. He had a way of looking around a room with his light brown eyes that said he was available for all sorts of mischief. If he ordered in, there was a good chance he'd attempt to seduce the deliveryman. Failing that, we had a couple of attractive neighbors, there were good-looking guys walking by on Aldine about every twenty minutes, and there were three gay bars within walking distance that might mistakenly serve the boy. I told him he was coming to dinner with me.

He answered with a contemptuous sigh.

Crawdaddy's was on Rush just above Hubbard. The neighborhood had once housed small factories that made things like shirts and sprockets. Now the old four-story brick buildings with large windows and open floor plans housed trendy restaurants and dance companies. The main change they'd made to the outside of the building, aside from simply cleaning it, was attaching a large pink neon sign, which scrawled Crawdaddy's in messy cursive across the second floor.

Terry and I walked in through the double doors of the main entrance. The kid wore his usual uniform of jeans, jean jacket, dangerously small Izod polo shirt, and a pair of red Crayons he'd found in the back of Brian's closet. Before we left the apartment he'd moussed his hair into a mushroom cloud. I'd learned not to react to whatever he did to himself for fear if I said anything it would just get worse.

Inside, the restaurant was a strange mix of glamour and New England seafood shanty. The lighting was low, reflecting off the freshly varnished wood-paneling on the walls and in the built-cabinets; the floor was done in two dark colors of shiny linoleum squares. Immediately in front of us stood a hostess stand with an attractive young woman behind it who probably modeled when she wasn't seating people. Several couples huddled anxiously around the podium, and it looked like Melody's roommate was right. It might be difficult to get a table. Terry, though, didn't seem to mind. He was less diffident than he had been in the cab, probably because he could see several attractive waiters scooting around the dining room.

When it was my turn, I was told there was a forty-five minute wait for a table.

"Would it be possible to have Melody wait on us?" I asked, hoping that it didn't increase the wait to two hours.

"Oh, Melody is working in the Blue Oyster Cafe."

"What's that?"

"It's our casual dining room. Just go right through that door and they may be able to seat you," she said, pointing at an arch that seemed to lead to a dead end.

But when I stepped into the arch I saw there were openings to either side. Terry and I went to our left and found ourselves standing in a large room dominated by an oyster bar. Mounds of crushed ice filled with dirty looking oysters seemed to spill off the bar. Booths lined the outer wall, while tall tables filled the floor space not occupied by the oyster bar. Both the booths and the tables were barstool height. Jazz played underneath the chatter of diners. It wasn't half bad. I think I recognized some Chick Corea followed by Miles Davis.

Another pretty hostess, more casually dressed than the first, approached us. I told her we wanted a table for two in Melody's section. She looked from me to Terry and then back again. Given the fact that it was a high-end restaurant, I figured most of the waiters in the main dining room were gay, which meant the hostess could probably figure out what Terry and I were. Well, Terry, at least. I wasn't wearing red shoes. In this girl's eyes, we were a man and his gay son or a gay man and his much younger lover. Either way there wasn't much connection to Melody. After all that flashed across her face, the girl led us to one of the raised booths by the windows.

While we were looking at the menu, which was extensive, I asked Terry one of a teenagers' most dreaded questions, "How's school?"

"Sucks."

"Are you passing all your classes?"

"I guess."

"Then it doesn't suck."

"What do you know about it?"

"I went to an all-boys Catholic high school. I have some idea what school is like for you."

Terry scowled. He didn't like being reminded that Brian and I understood what he'd been through, that we'd been through similar things. Since we'd become his unofficial parents, well Brian more than me, he'd transferred the thinly veiled contempt he had for his real parents to us. Or maybe like most teenagers he was half psychopath.

"You only have a little more than two years and you're done."

"Fuck. Two whole years."

I almost told him a year wasn't very long, but I remembered the way time was different for kids; remembered summers that seemed to last forever, and the disappointment when they didn't. A waitress came over. She was well past thirty, thin, wore too much make-up, and had faded eyes that sunk into her skull. Her uniform was a tuxedo shirt and a blue jean mini-skirt. She wore her blond hair long, pulling it back into a ponytail with a ball of curls in the front. The hairstyle was pretty similar to the one her sister had worn to trial.

She gave us an over-animated smile and said, "Hi! I'm Melody. Cathy says you asked for me? Was I recommended?"

"In a way," I said. Which might have been mean. "I'm working for your sister's attorney. I need to ask you a few questions."

"Um...I'm at work."

"I'm also hungry. Thought I'd kill two birds with one stone."

"Can I get you something from the bar," she asked, obviously trying to wrest control of the situation away from me.

"I'll have a Bacardi and Coke," Terry said.

"He'll have a Coke," I corrected. "I'll have a Johnnie Walker Red with soda, and I'd like to know why your parents are refusing to testify on your sister's behalf during sentencing."

"They loved Wes. More than Maddy, if you ask her."

"You didn't love Wes?" I asked before she could slip away.

"He was a fake. I knew that before she married him. He was the kind of guy who knew what people wanted to hear and managed to say it at just the right time."

"What about your brother? He won't testify either."

"He does what he's told." There was a bitterness in her voice that slowed my next question enough for her to say, "Let me get your drinks," and walk away.

"She thinks you're an asshole," Terry said. The kid was more observant than I thought.

"I'll leave her a big tip." I took out my cigarettes and shook one out of the box. Terry snatched one for himself before I had a chance to say anything. I wouldn't have said anything, though. Brian didn't like him smoking, didn't like him swearing for that matter, but I decided to let the minor infractions go and focus on the big stuff. If we kept him alive and out of prison until he was eighteen then we could tackle the small stuff.

"How's your love life?" I asked.

"What love life? You keep ruining it."

That was the answer I was hoping for. I even hoped it was true.

"What about the boys at school? At least a couple of them must be gay."

"So you're saying I can have sex with kids but not grownups?" The way he exhaled his cigarette smoke made it look like he was trying to put out a fire. "That's perverted."

"I'm not saying you can have sex with anyone." I tried to remember if it was actually legal for kids to have sex with each other. I suspected it wasn't. It was just one of those things that happened so often there was no way to arrest and prosecute the guilty. And beyond that, which kid would you prosecute? Or would you send both to prison? I shook those thoughts off and said, "I'm trying to say that if you liked a boy at school and wanted to hang out with him in his parents' cellar or someplace, then Brian and I wouldn't worry too much about it."

"Brian would. He'd want me to use a fucking condom."

That was an unavoidable truth. Brian had read a brochure some guys in New York had put together that suggested fucking with condoms. It seemed kind of pointless to me but Brian was gung ho, even going so far as to bother Howard Brown about putting out a similar brochure. They hadn't succumbed yet, but knowing Brian they would eventually.

Melody came back with our drinks.

I stubbed out my cigarette and asked, "Did you know about your brother-in-law's affair?"

"No one knew."

"Do you think your sister's lying about that?"

"No. I know my sister. She'd never tell a lie that didn't make her look good."

"So if she was lying what would she say?"

"I don't know. Like he beat her, I guess. Something that really made her look like a victim."

"Did he beat her?"

"No. He wasn't that kind of asshole."

"What kind of asshole was he?"

"The loser kind. He almost never had a job, and when he did he spent all the money on himself. He was a selfish prick and my sister should have dumped him a long time ago. Are you ready to order?"

"Um, yeah, sure. Terry do you know what you want?"

"I'll have a cheeseburger."

"It's a seafood restaurant. Try some kind of fish."

"Fish is gross."

I gave up. "I'll have the fried shrimp." Which wasn't any healthier than a cheeseburger but I couldn't get it at a thousand other restaurants in Chicago.

Melody grabbed the menus and walked away as quickly as she could.

I looked at Terry a moment and then asked, "Have you been staying away from the personals?"

"Don't do that."

"What?"

"Treat me like someone you're investigating."

Apparently my interrogation skills left a little to be desired.

"Are you happy you're not testifying in the DeCarlo trial?" The week before an ASA had called to tell Terry he wouldn't be testifying. DeCarlo had traded sex for better grades with a number of boys in Terry's class, boys who were more visibly upset by it than Terry.

"That's still a question," he pointed out.

"Questions are a normal part of conversation. How am I going to know how you are unless I ask questions?" He didn't respond so I continued, "You don't want to testify. It's not very much fun."

"You had to testify?"

"Couple of times when I was a police officer. Domestic abuse cases mostly."

"I don't hate him. That's why they don't want me to testify."

That was absolutely true. I didn't know what to say. We'd skirted around this before. I knew that Owen, his attorney, had explained what consent meant legally and that what Deacon DeCarlo had done was wrong, no matter whether the boys agreed or not. But still, he had some trouble with the concept—which is probably why it's a good idea that sixteen-year-olds can't legally have sex. Of course, all of this was complicated by his being an emancipated minor, meaning that he was an adult and could consent to just about anything except the one thing he really wanted to get busy consenting to.

Finally, I said, "You don't have to hate anybody you don't want to."

I gave him a bit of time to see if he wanted to talk about this anymore, but he didn't so I cut him a break and asked, "So what is it you like so much about the games you're playing on the TV?"

He spent the next five minutes explaining the awesomeness of *Pac-Man*. I smoked another cigarette, managing not to give him one. He was explaining the idea of leveling-up when our meals arrived. Melody laid them out on the table and, when she was done, dutifully asked, "Is there anything else I can get you?"

Dipping a crusty shrimp into the surprisingly good tartar sauce, I asked, "Do you have any idea who your brother-in-law was sleeping with?"

"You asked me that."

"No, I asked if you knew about the affair. Now, I'm asking if you've figured out who the affair might have been with."

"Not a clue."

"Did your sister really think she could collect on the insurance after she killed him?"

Melody almost laughed. "No. That was the stupidest part of the trial. Maddy didn't even want to buy that insurance. It was all Wes's idea. I mean it made sense to get insurance on Maddy, if something happened to her they were screwed, but him? He didn't even have a job. If he died she'd actually save money." She thought about what she'd just said and added, "I mean, if he'd died in a normal way. Anyway, it was weird that he wanted it so bad."

"Why didn't that come up at the trial?" I asked, putting a shrimp on Terry's plate and earning myself a nasty look.

"It did come up. The agent said that he'd talked to Wes mostly but when he tried to say it was Wes's idea to buy the insurance there were all these objections. Wes was dead so who could say whether it was his idea or not, you know?" I was chewing on a delicious shrimp so I wasn't too fast with the next question. "Is that it?" she asked. "I have other tables, you know."

With my mouth half full I asked, "Why is your last name Oddy?" It was just idle curiosity, but she wasn't wearing a wedding ring.

"I was married long time ago. Before Maddy even. Guy was a jerk. Same kind of jerk as Wes."

"But you kept his name?"

"I liked the way it sounded."

Before we left Crawdaddy's I gave Melody a fifty percent tip and got her to look at the remaining names on my list. She filled in few holes for me. The remaining people testifying for Madeline were her hygienist and one of her patients. Refusing to testify were her dental partner, a Dr. Caspian; the office manager, Cynthia Furlong; and two odd names. One was a woman named Emily Fante, who Melody was unfamiliar with, and the other was one of Madeline's high school teachers, Roland Bowen. Melody seemed unhappy that there were things about her sister she didn't know and, despite the generous tip, we left her in a bad mood.

When we got home, I insisted we watch TV instead of allowing Terry to play his game, while I slouched on the settee waiting for him to go to bed. *Coal Miner's Daughter* was the Monday Night Movie, and I would have changed the channel but we were already past the part where a fourteen-year-old girl marries a grown man and nobody blinks an eye. I had the feeling that wasn't the kind of thing I should be showing Terry and was glad I didn't have to.

Toward the end of the movie, I fell asleep and woke up when Brian came through the door. He seemed surprised to see us in his living room, though it wasn't quite ten o'clock. Behind him was a young man of about twenty-five with strong facial features he hadn't yet grown into. He was nearly as tall as I was, and so thin I wondered if he'd fall over in the wind.

"This is Franklin," Brian said. "Franklin Eggers."

There wasn't a reason in the world Terry and I needed to know this guy's last name if he was just a trick, so he wasn't. He was more than that. Franklin smiled in an insincere way and Brian made an awkward stab at explaining who Terry and I were. "Terry's parents threw him out and Nick's staying here for a while."

I decided it might be a good idea to start looking for an apartment in the morning.

Chapter Three

That next day, I was up and out before anyone else woke up. On the corner of Brian's block there's a fancy coffee place where I would have loved to pick up a cup, but they didn't open until seven so I swung down to the White Hen on Belmont. It was a long walk, so I had plenty of time to think. I decided to split the day in half. I'd spend the morning on Madeline's case and the afternoon on Jimmy's. I went over my conversation with Melody. I wasn't sure I learned anything of value other than that she believed there was a mistress. She had no idea who that mistress might be. Would anyone else know?

When I got to my office, the coffee was cold and the bear claw stale, though in its defense the pastry was stale when I bought it. While I chewed, I pulled out the Chicago Greater Metropolitan Phonebook and looked up Emily Fante. There were about twelve Fante's. None of them Emily. I called them all and asked those who'd answer the phone if they knew an Emily. None of them did. I was looking for a woman named Emily Fante who didn't seem to be related to any of the Fantes in Chicago. She must be from somewhere else originally, I thought, though it was hardly useful.

I followed the same procedure for Roland Bowen, who also wasn't listed. I thought it was a strong possibility that he lived in the suburbs. Most of them were included in the Metro phonebook. But if he taught Madeline as a teenager that meant he was teaching in Park Ridge. I'd been to Park Ridge and knew it was a pricey suburb surrounded by several less pricey suburbs. As a teacher, it was unlikely that he lived in Park Ridge itself. I guessed he could have lived a half an hour to forty minutes further west, which might have put him into a different phonebook. Or, like Emily Fante, he had an unlisted number.

I suppose I could have dialed information and started guessing at which northwestern suburb he might live in, but instead I decided I'd take the easy way out and flipped to the yellow pages. I looked up dentists and found the number for Caspian Levine Dental Care. I patiently waited until the clock clicked eight and dialed the number. Unfortunately, I got their answering service and was told the office didn't open until nine. Given people's work schedules I suspected that there were appointments available before nine, so the office was open. They just weren't answering the phone.

I turned on my radio and switched to a jazz station I liked. The news was still on and I learned that tensions in the Middle East were high now that Passover had begun, the Vice President was in Geneva working on disarming the Russians, and an announcement was expected soon as to the cause of AIDS which, according to the newscast, was some kind of cancer virus. That wasn't too far off from the information in the brochure Brian picked up in New York, *How to Have Sex in an Epidemic*. In fact, I gathered from Brian that people had been saying it might be a virus for almost a year. But that didn't make a lot of sense to me. A cold was a virus. If AIDS traveled like a cold, then why didn't everyone have it? Unless, it was a virus that worked more like mononucleosis? Mono was called the kissing disease, but did it really transfer that way? Is that how AIDS transferred? Through deep kissing? No, probably not. If it were we'd have an even bigger mess on our hands.

Feeling lazy, I shoved the phonebook back in its drawer and called directory assistance. I asked for a number for Herb Dotson in Skokie. It wasn't listed. I tried Lana Shepherd in Skokie but got nothing. In Chicago, the operator found an L. Shepherd on Lake Shore Drive. I took that number. Then something occurred to me. Something that should have occurred to me right off the bat. I hung up and dialed Cooke, Babcock and Lackerby. Owen Lovejoy, Esquire picked up his own telephone. It was still too early for a secretary to be there.

"Question. Why did you give me a sheet of names without phone numbers?"

"Oh, sorry. It's the list that we're preparing for the State's Attorney. We don't want to give them too much."

"But I'm not the State's Attorney."

"Yes, but you do know how to find people without phone numbers, don't you?"

"Absolutely. I just hate billing you to get information you already had."

I felt like I was fighting with him and I didn't want to be. I decided to throw him a bone and said, "I already talked to Melody Oddy."

And of course, that was the wrong thing to say. "Sweetheart, I asked you to work on the other side of the list first. Did you not hear me?"

"Yeah, but Melody works in a restaurant and I was hungry."

I could almost hear him shaking his head. "Well did you find anything out?"

"She gave me an idea why her parents won't testify, which I wanted before I go see them." I let the idea that I might know what I was doing sink in, then I asked, "Look, you know more than I do about all of this. Let me ask you a few questions before I run off and start bothering people."

"I have five minutes then I'm in a meeting."

"I'll be quick then. Who's Emily Fante?"

"Oh, that's right…I should have mentioned her to you. Sorry. She's a friend of Madeline's, but when I brought up the name she wanted her taken off the list."

"Madeline wanted her off the list? So why is she on the list?"

"It bugged me that she wanted her off. Melody was so sure she'd be helpful."

"Melody? Melody gave you the name?"

"Yes."

That didn't fit but I decided to hold off a moment. "Did you talk to Emily about testifying?" I asked.

"No. I left her a message and then when I called back again the phone had been shut off. I haven't had a chance to ask Melody if she's got the new number."

"Melody says she doesn't know Emily Fante."

"Oh? That's rather curious."

I was tempted to say "quite" as though I was in some English drawing room mystery, but instead I said, "It might not mean anything. Melody may have thought the woman was a friend and then found out she wasn't."

"Then why not tell you that? You should find Emily Fante and talk to her."

"Do you think she's the mistress?"

"At the moment, dear, I don't know anything more about Emily Fante than you do."

"All right. What about the high school teacher? Do you think he's important?"

"No, I don't. They spent a lot of time trying to make Madeline look stupid enough to murder for insurance she couldn't possibly claim. I think she just wanted someone to testify that she's smart."

"But he won't?"

"He sounded pretty old when I talked to him. I don't think he actually remembers her."

"Do you remember where he lives? I couldn't get his number."

"Oh, I don't. It's really far though…look, I really do need to go now. We'll talk later, all right?"

I agreed and hung up. I had a decision to make. I could continue with my morning as I'd planned it or I could drop everything and focus on finding Emily Fante. I decided to stick with my plan. I could drop it later if I got more information on the Fante woman.

Since it was after nine, I called Dr. Caspian's office again. A woman answered with a cheerful, "Caspian Dental Group." They'd changed the name. I wondered if they even bothered to wait until the guilty verdict came in.

"Could I speak to Cynthia Furlong?"

"Speaking."

"This Nick Nowak, I'm working with Madeline Levine-Berkson's attorneys on her sentencing. Do you have a few moments?"

"No. But I imagine you'll just call back."

"Yes, I will, I'm afraid."

She sighed as though she spent her entire day talking to annoying private detectives. "Look, I've already said I won't testify for her, so why are you calling?"

"I'd like to know why you won't testify for her."

"She killed her husband. She should go to prison for that."

"The sentencing hearing isn't about whether or not she'll go to prison. It's about how long she'll go to prison. She could go to prison for twenty years. That's a very long time." It seemed wise not to mention four years of probation was also a possibility.

There was silence on the other end of the phone. I could hear another line ring in the background. She said, "Hold on a second," and was gone. The radio played Marvin Gaye. They'd been doing that a lot, even though I wouldn't exactly call him a jazz musician. I guess when you're shot by your own father people are willing to stretch a point. Finally, Cynthia came back. "Look, Dr. Levine-

Berkson has hurt a lot people and I think she deserves whatever she gets. Now, if you'll excuse—"

"Two quick questions. Do you know a woman named Emily Fante?"

"Maybe. I don't know. Dr. Levine-Berkson got personal calls from someone named Emily. She never left a last name."

"Do you know anything about their relationship?"

"Relationship? Dr. Levine-Berkson was a lot of things but she was *not* a lesbian." The distain she threw onto the word lesbian suggested she thought sapphic affection was a far worse crime than killing your husband.

"People have friendships. People have business relationships. People even have relatives. Was this Emily woman any of those?"

"I'm sure I don't know."

"All right. Is Kimmy Crete there? I'd like to talk to her."

"Kimmy doesn't work here anymore. And that's it. I'm not saying anything else. Goodbye Mister... I've forgotten your name. Don't call back." And with that she hung up on me. I was left with an unsettling thought. How exactly had Madeline hurt the people she worked with?

I smoked a couple of cigarettes, finished my very cold coffee, and dialed Nan Dotson. According to Melody she was a neighbor of her sister's in Skokie where the Levine-Berksons lived. The phone was answered and someone said "Hello." I thought it must be a child since the voice was high pitched so I said, "Hello. I'm calling for Mrs. Dotson."

"Speaking," the child said.

I forged on. "Mrs. Dotson, this is Nick Nowak, I'm working with Cooke, Babcock and Lackerby on Madeline Levine-Berkson's case." That was a mouthful.

"Yes."

"I understand that you're going to testify in support of Ms. Levine-Berkson."

"Yes, I am. Absolutely."

"So you know her well?"

"Well? I wouldn't say *well*. I mean, our kids know each other. She's a good neighbor." Madeline was going to need more help than someone saying she's a good neighbor.

"And her husband? Was he a good neighbor?"

"I guess. He was…" She hesitated. I could almost hear her thinking that she'd gotten in over her head.

"He was what?"

"Sneaky. He was always coming and going at strange hours. Not that that means anything. It was just…different."

"Do you know anything about the woman he was having an affair with?"

"I thought I just had to say that Madeline was nice." Somehow her voice managed to sound even younger.

"So you do know who Wes was having an affair with?"

"No. I don't. I mean, I might. I'm not sure. I think I saw her. Once. I have an image of him with a very tall, very thin, dark-haired woman. But I can't really remember when I saw them together."

"You're sure it wasn't Madeline. Doesn't she have dark hair?"

"Yes, I know her hair is dark. Underneath. She always dyes it blond. Besides, she's short and a little, well, chubby around the hips. This woman was rail thin." Then she added, "My husband is going to be so mad at me."

"Why is that?"

"This has been really hard on him."

"Has it?" I could see how it was hard on Madeline. How it was hard on her kids. How it was hard on her family. And especially how it was hard on Wes. But I didn't exactly see how it was hard on their insurance agent. "Your husband sold them a policy?"

"He feels bad about the things he had to say. They were true. But he felt bad anyway."

"I wasn't at the trial."

"Oh, God. They made it look all wrong. Madeline and Wes just wanted to protect their children. That's why people buy insurance, isn't it?"

I had no idea why people bought insurance. I had none. Still, I made a reassuring sound, "Mmhhmm."

"Anyway, I'm hoping that I can make up for what he said. At least a little."

"But your husband's mad about that?"

"He just wants it to be over."

"Did Madeline ever mention someone named Emily Fante?"

"Who's that?"

"No one important. So, Wes Berkson came and went at odd hours. Can you tell me more than that?"

"I don't know what you're asking, exactly."

Neither did I. I was fishing. "You heard a noise late at night and looked out the window and saw Berkson coming home late. Is that the kind of thing you mean?"

"Sometimes late at night, sometimes in the middle of the day. It never made any sense."

"He couldn't have gotten some funky, off-hours job?"

"He didn't dress for any kind of job I've ever heard of."

"How did he dress?"

"Wrong usually. He'd wear a windbreaker in the middle of winter and a sweater in the middle of summer. He was always in jeans and sneakers. But not nice jeans, dirty jeans."

"And not nice sneakers either?"

"No. The canvas kind."

What did that mean? I wondered. Did it mean anything? It sounded like he didn't have any money. That went just fine with his not having a job, but not so well with his being married to a dentist. His wife must have given him money. But when she did, he didn't spend it on clothes. So what did he do with it? And he seemed impervious to the weather. Or at least unaware of it.

"Is that all? How was he with the kids?"

"Erratic. Sometimes he was the best dad ever and then other times he didn't seem to want anything to do with them."

I couldn't think of anything else to ask. I was too distracted by something that had occurred to me. There may have been another woman, but there was also a lot more to this and I wasn't sure yet exactly what that was. Before I hung up I mentioned that I might like to talk to her again. In her little girl voice she said she'd better not. I said I understood and crossed my fingers that I hadn't just managed to discourage one of the few people willing to talk on Madeline's behalf.

I pulled out my portable typewriter and spent an hour typing up my notes. I was out of the habit of writing reports. For my investigation into Operation Tea and Crumpets I was prohibited from writing them, so my reports for the Levine-Berkson case would be the first I'd done in almost a year and a half. I debated with myself about how much information I should include about my interview with Melody Oddy, since I'd already discussed it with Owen, but then I remembered that he dealt with hundreds of details every day, he might need to look at the report to remember what he already knew. I tried to put down everything I could think of about that interview and the two short ones I'd conducted over the phone. By the time I was done I had three double-spaced pages. As things became clearer I'd type them up so they were less random and made more sense.

It was almost lunchtime, so I decided to call Lana Shepherd and arrange to meet her. As Madeline's best friend she was likely to have as much information as her sister, possibly more. I expected the interview to be rather long. When I called I got an answering machine.

"Hi, this is Nick Nowak. I'm working on your friend Madeline's case. I'd like to meet with you and ask a few questions." I left her my office number and said I hoped to hear from her soon.

I'd hung up and begun to think about where I wanted to go for lunch when there was a knock on my door. I'd never had my name put on the door so it was always a little disconcerting when someone arrived that way. It meant they'd had to find the street address, figure out that the unmarked door downstairs led somewhere, climb the stairs, glance at the two other doors on the second floor, both of which featured the names of their occupants, and then take a chance on the blank door.

Despite the fact that it could be anyone on the other side, including some lawless nutcase with a gun, I yelled, "Come in."

The door opened a bit tentatively and there was Father Joseph Biernacki. He wore civilian clothes—jeans and a button down shirt with a windbreaker—rather than the traditional black suit and white collar people still expected from a priest. His hair was red-ish brown and he'd let it grow out a bit; he smiled at me, showing his broken tooth, making his fair skin crinkle around the eyes. His nose, cheeks, neck, and what I could see of his chest through his open collar, were all spattered with freckles. Freckles that made me think of Jackson Pollack paintings, of constellations and star maps, of unknown geographies I wanted to explore.

"How did you find me?" I asked.

"You gave me your card."

"Oh. Okay. Why are you here?"

"It's lunchtime." He blushed and I watched the redness spread across his cheeks, and neck, and chest.

"You came by to have lunch with me? You know my phone number is on that card, too."

"I was afraid you'd say no." He was a smart guy, I probably would have. I liked him. I just didn't like complicated. And what could be more complicated than a priest?

"All right. So let's have lunch."

I stood up, grabbed my cigarettes, pulled my overcoat off the back of my chair and slipped it on. I took the few steps to the door, but he was blocking the way. I was a few inches away from him, close enough to smell the lavender soap he'd showered with, when he said, "There's something I should tell you."

"What is that?"

"I've left the church. Or rather, I'm leaving the church. They've asked that I consider my decision for six months, that I pray—"

I leaned forward and kissed him gently, carefully, as though he were a wild animal who might bolt at any sudden movement. And then, after a long moment, he did bolt. He rested a hand on my chest and eased me back. "That isn't why I came."

"Isn't it?"

"Maybe it is. I don't know. I hoped we'd talk."

"You don't have to leave the priesthood to talk to me, you know."

"I know that. Maybe I don't mean only talk. But you need to be careful with me. Slow."

I had no idea if I could do that, no idea if I even wanted to.

Chapter Four

A cold drizzle fell as we walked down Clark to El Jardin, and I squeezed under an umbrella with Joseph. There were closer places to eat, but, regardless of how this conversation went, I felt like I was going to need a drink and a frozen margarita sounded appealing. A sudden burst of white adobe announced that El Jardin occupied the first floor of a three-story brick building. A large patio—*jardin* is probably garden in Spanish after all—ran along the side of the building. It was empty and wet.

Inside, Joseph and I were situated at a small table against the wall. Without asking if he wanted one, I ordered us two frozen margaritas with salt. A busboy brought a plastic bowl of chips and I nibbled while I stared at Joseph. He hadn't said much of anything on the walk down. Other than asking me how I was, to which I was able to honestly reply, "Good. Very good."

"I feel like I have something to do with your decision," I said when the margaritas arrived. "Or am I flattering myself."

"When you and I broke into the rectory. I realized afterward that I probably wanted to get caught. I wanted to be kicked out."

"So, I don't have much to do with it?"

He smiled. "You do, I suppose. You're a very tempting guy."

"I don't feel like a tempting guy," I said, because I didn't. I knew guys liked me but I wasn't always sure why. Lately, I was thin and disheveled, with dark brown hair that needed trimming, an unremarkable face that needed shaving, and hazel-colored eyes that could use a good dose of Visine.

"That's probably part of your appeal. You have the confidence to just be you." A twinkle lit up his face. "Or maybe it's that you look like you rolled about of bed and might roll back in at any moment."

He was being more flirtatious than I wanted him to be at the beginning of the meal. If he kept it up, I'd be grabbing him and pulling him to the ground, which would get us thrown out of the restaurant and possibly into jail. I changed the subject. "Did you like being a priest?"

"Most of the time, yes. A lot, actually."

"Have you considered becoming Episcopalian? I hear it's almost the same thing."

"I think my central problem is a problem wherever I go."

Off the top of my head, I couldn't think of any churches that equated sucking cock with being Christ-like. "You're probably right. You said you'll be considering your decision for six months. What does that entail?"

"Prayer. Counseling. Meditation."

"I assume you've had sex with men before. Have you ever felt anything stronger than lust?"

"Actually, I haven't had sex with a man. I *have* had feelings stronger than lust, though."

I took a long gulp of margarita. This wasn't making sense. "How old are you?"

"Nearly thirty."

"Have you ever had sex with a woman?"

"No. I was a very devout teenager, altar boy, bible study, Catholic boys' school, followed by seminary and the priesthood." There must have been a dubious look on my face because he added, "I know that things happen in boys' school and seminary, I just managed to avoid them. They frightened me. Still do, I suppose."

"So then how can you make a decision if you've never tried anything? I mean, it would be awful to leave the priesthood and find out later you don't like sucking cock."

Unfortunately, the waiter chose that moment to return for our order. There was a devilish smirk on Joseph's face as he looked down at his menu. I wondered how he did that, how he seemed devilish when he had no firsthand knowledge of sin. I wondered if he was telling me the complete truth. He ordered a chilé relleno and I had a combination lunch, which included an enchilada, a taco and a tostada.

When the waiter left, I stared at Joseph, waiting for him to answer my question. It didn't seem wise to repeat it. Finally, he started, "It's not like ice cream. You don't have to try every single kind to decide which is your favorite. I'm not worried about whether I'll like sucking cock. If I love someone I'm sure I'll like it just fine."

"It's not always about love," I pointed out. "Sometimes it's about sex."

"What did Oscar Wilde say about sex? 'Everything is about sex, except sex which is about power.' I may be paraphrasing."

"I think you may be wandering off topic," I said as I finished my drink. I hoped the waiter would come back soon and offer me another.

"All sex is about love in some way. Even if it's only love of mankind."

"You're not afraid of finding out you and mankind might just be friends?"

"No. I love mankind."

We fell into staring at each other until I was completely uncomfortable.

"You said I have to be careful with you. What did that mean?"

"I don't know. If I knew I wouldn't have needed to say it."

I had the feeling I should get up and leave him there. This wasn't going to end well and I knew it. But then I thought, what relationship does end well? Things didn't end well with Daniel—any of the times it ended—and things certainly didn't end well with Harker. I tried to think of a relationship that had ended well and I couldn't. Each time I thought I had, my relationship with Brian for instance, I had to be honest with myself and admit that the relationship hadn't really ended at all. The only relationships I could think of that had truly ended well were the ones where I hadn't bothered to ask for a name.

"This conversation is far too serious," Joseph said out of the blue. "Tell me how you are. Tell me you're happy and that things are good with you."

"I'm working a lot. And I'm liking that."

"What are you working on?"

"I can't discuss my work. My clients expect a certain amount of discretion."

"Really? You talked to me freely about your work at St. Boniface."

"That was different. I was interviewing you, for one thing. And I needed your help."

"Can't you deputize me or something? I'm still a priest. We do secrets pretty well, you know."

"If I need you, I'll let you know."

In point of fact, Joseph knew things about me that could send me to prison for a very long time. It wasn't a question of trust. I trusted him. Gossiping about my clients was a bad idea though. I could however gossip about myself, so I told him about my living arrangement and my un-official, half-assed parenting of Terry Winkler.

"I wish I had more experience with teenagers," he said, then corrected himself, "I didn't mean that the way it sounded. I wish I knew more about them."

"They're not that difficult, they're just adults with some parts missing." I don't know why I said that; I didn't have the slightest idea what to do with Terry. I wondered why I wanted to impress Joseph with my so-called parenting skills.

"So, your friend Brian, you're not boyfriends?"

"No. We've fooled around. I guess he's kind of a fuck buddy."

"Fuck buddy?"

"Oh, you don't know that term? Well, it's a friend—"

"You don't have to explain. It's vividly self-explanatory."

I mentally kicked myself. Did I really think a priest wasn't going to be at least a little bit judgmental about the way guys behaved? Worse than just a priest, too. A virgin priest. His idea of what a relationship with a man should be like was probably something out of a Harlequin romance—but with a sex change for the heroine. Or some queer version of *Father Knows Best*, co-starring Robert Young and Ozzie Nelson without their bland little wives.

Our lunches arrived. I ordered another margarita. Joseph wasn't even halfway through his. We took a few bites and agreed the food was good. Halfway through I asked, "Do you not have any gay friends?"

"I do. A couple. We just don't discuss anything directly." He made me think of priests sitting around drinking cognac while discussing Oscar Wilde and the joys of male companionship. "They're not very happy people," he added, destroying my little picture.

I made short work of my dinner and pushed my plate away.

"I think Brian may have met someone. He brought this guy home last night; he was still there in the morning."

"That bothers you?"

"Not for me. Brian was with my friend Ross." I decided to leave out the part where Ross was also a fuck buddy of mine. It was a confusing enough conversation. "Ross moved downstate to be with his family. He's dying of AIDS."

"And he didn't want to be a burden to Brian?"

"His parents are bible-thumpers. He thinks God is going to save him."

"God *will* save him. Though probably not the way he's hoping."

"Does God ever give people exactly what they want?"

"You're thinking of Santa Claus. God gives us what we need."

"I can't say I believe that."

"What do you believe?"

"Human beings are attracted to patterns. We find them everywhere, even where they don't exist. We make stories out of them."

"Which is the way God made us."

"You know, you have the same first name as the man I killed. Is that coincidence or God's plan?"

"If God created everything, then God created coincidence. Nothing is outside God's plan."

"So you're saying that God wrote the rules of nature and then tossed in a healthy dose of coincidence. Why would he do that?"

"To keep things interesting."

My second margarita arrived and I realized I didn't want it. Something about the idea of coincidence keeping things interesting wasn't sitting well with me. Coincidence was all well and good when you happened to run into a friend you'd just been thinking about on the street, but illness was also a coincidence, AIDS was a coincidence, and that wasn't making me especially fond of a God who'd create it.

"Is something wrong?" Joseph asked.

"I shouldn't have ordered a second drink."

"Leave it."

"It was four bucks."

"It's on me. I'm still getting my salary while I think things over."

I was a little embarrassed. Money was fine; I shouldn't have said anything about the price of the drink. I could afford it. I could afford the whole lunch, and if I'd been a little faster on the uptake would have offered to treat him. But he had shown up out of the blue so I decided to let him pay. I'd treat him next time. If there was a next time, and the longer we talked the more I thought there shouldn't be.

On the walk back to my office it was raining harder and we had to be even more careful to stay under the umbrella. To distract us from the fact that we were pressed against each other, Joseph asked me questions. Of course, the fact that the questions were about my sex life defeated the purpose. There wasn't a whole lot to say about my sex life until Daniel came along. There had been a few experiences with other men, furtive, dangerous, exciting, but also disappointing. And, like a good Catholic boy, I'd tried dating women. Which was how I'd come to meet Daniel. I'd dated his sister. Briefly and unsuccessfully.

"And you knew it was love right away?"

"No. I knew he was damned attractive and I was happy when I was with him. Love is more complicated than that."

He nodded and said, "Yes, I think you're right."

When we reached my door, we walked through the downstairs door, shook out the umbrella and closed it, as we were about to climb the stairs he said, "Wait. I'd better not come up."

"All right. So we'll say goodbye here then?" I suspected he wanted to kiss, but because I'd kissed him earlier, I decided to make him be the one to initiate. I waited. Listening to him breathing. Finally he exhaled and leaned into me. His kiss was gentle, as mine had been, his tongue tentatively exploring me. Without thinking, I pulled him against me. I wanted to feel the weight of his body against mine. I slipped my hands into his jacket and felt his strong back beneath the cotton of his shirt.

He kissed me a little longer and then pushed away. "I should go."

"Are you sure? We could go upstairs to my office."

"No. I have a lot to think about."

I reached down and grabbed his dick. It was as hard as I thought it would be. He exhaled roughly. "It feels like you've already made a decision."

"Play nice."

"Never," I said, but took my hand away.

"I need to go," he said.

"Confession?"

"Maybe later. I'd like to see you again."

"Sure, just give me a call." I wasn't entirely sure I meant it.

"How about Thursday night. Dinner. Maybe a movie."

"What's wrong with tomorrow?"

"Too soon."

"And Friday?'

"Too far away." He kissed me again. "Say yes."

"All right. Yes."

A moment later he was gone. I climbed the stairs to my office, stretched out on the sofa, and quickly jerked off before the feel of his lips on mine left completely. Then I promptly fell asleep.

It was late afternoon when the phone rang, waking me. The sun was easing its way down to the western horizon, leaving the city dim and shadowy. The clock radio said it was five-thirty-four. I stumbled the few feet to my desk, mainly because I'd neglected to pull up my pants, and grabbed for the phone.

"Hello?" I said, my voice a sleepy foghorn.

"Oh, hi, is this Nick Nowak?"

"Yes, it is."

"This is Lana Shepherd. You called me?"

"Yes, I did. I'm working with Cooke, Babcock and Lackerby on your friend Madeline's case."

"Yes, you said that in your message. Is this about my testimony? Because I have an appointment day after tomorrow to go over it."

"This is different. I'm hoping you can lead me to other possibilities for helpful testimony." That was about the shortest way I could think of to explain what I was up to. "I'm hoping you can spend a half an hour with me, maybe a little longer?"

"All right. I just got off work and I don't feel like going out. Can you come here?"

"Probably. Where is here?"

She gave me an address on Lake Shore Drive just above Belmont. I'd lucked out. She could have been anywhere in the Chicago area, but she happened to be within walking distance of my office. I told her I could be there in less than half an hour and she said that would be fine. I hung up the phone and pulled up my pants.

Chapter Five

Lana Shepherd's building was at 3220 Lake Shore Drive; actually it was two buildings that shared a lobby and a truncated courtyard with the addresses 3210 and 3220. Both were fifteen stories tall, made of red brick, and had broad windows for the living rooms, narrower windows for the bedrooms, and very tiny windows for the bathrooms. They were built sometime in the 1950s and the architecture did a brilliant job of capturing the malaise of the period. Over the entrance, metal letters spelled out the words Two Towers.

The buildings on either side dwarfed Two Towers in architectural grandeur, if not height. The building across Melrose was defiantly mod and rose to thirty stories. The building on the northern side wasn't as tall but it took up the rest of the block. It was nearly a hundred years old and very likely featured butler's pantries larger than the bedrooms in Two Towers.

I'd been expecting someplace hoity-toity given the Lake Shore Drive address, but the building was decidedly middle class. I wondered what Lana Shepherd did for a living and how she'd come to live in the building. She lived in the north tower, though honestly I felt a little silly thinking of a fifteen-story building as a tower. The Sears Tower was a tower. The Hancock was a tower. Anything with less than fifty floors seemed far too short to be a tower, at least in Chicago.

The lobby was spacious and clean with simple leather furniture. In the middle was an unoccupied desk with a sign sitting on it that said the rental office was open from ten to seven; below that information an arrow pointed to the south tower. At either end of the lobby were identical security doors and intercom systems. Fortunately, Lana had said she was in 407, so I didn't have to go searching through nearly a hundred names looking for her name. I pressed the right button and a half a minute later the security door in front of me buzzed.

I took the elevator to the fourth floor and wandered around the halls until I found her door. The apartment was situated at the back corner of the building facing north and west. When Lana opened the door, I saw that she was an attractive woman in her early thirties. She wore a pair of designer jeans and a fitted T-shirt. The apartment was very warm so she hadn't bothered with shoes or socks. Her hair was cut short and she'd died it carrot red.

She invited me into the living room which was to the left of the front door, the main window faced west and I had the immediate feeling that the window in the bedroom, to my right as I walked in, likely had a dismal view of the classic brick building next door. She had a large brown plaid sofa with an antique trunk sitting in front of it as a coffee table. In front of the long window stretched a dining table and six chairs. It was far too big for the apartment and had either come from her family or a grander part of her life. The kitchen was behind a folding door and included a narrow stove, a miniature refrigerator, and a small sink unit. I liked the apartment and said so.

She waved me off. "The nice ones are in the front. They have lake views. Would you like a pop or something?"

"Water would be fine, thanks."

It took only a moment for her to step over to the tiny kitchen, grab a glass from the cupboard, and fill it with water. When she came back into the living room we sat down on the sofa.

"I don't really understand why you're here," she said.

"I'm looking for things that might help Madeline. Things people might not think of. Maybe we should start with Madeline's parents and brother. They've refused to testify. Do you know why?"

"I don't know for sure, but I think it has to do with the kids. Hedy dotes on them. I don't think she wants Madeline to get them back. Ever."

"Hedy?"

"Mrs. Levine."

"Why wouldn't she want her daughter to have her own children?"

"Well, she did murder their father."

"I know, but the reaction is more like something you'd expect from his parents, not hers."

"There's a lot of history."

"That's what I'm here for. It's the history that might be helpful."

"No. It wouldn't be," she said simply and picked up a cola drink she'd left on the trunk. She sipped it carefully then looked back at me.

I took a moment deciding whether to press her on that. My guess was that whatever she was holding back would be very helpful. Finally, I asked, "What did you think of Wes Berkson?"

"He was an asshole."

"So I've heard."

"He was the kind of guy who was always on the hustle. Always had a scheme he was working. Things would be better as soon as he put some deal together. Somehow the deals never came together. He asked me for money about at least dozen times. From ten bucks to ten thousand."

"He asked you for ten thousand dollars?"

"My mother died. He knew I was going to get a little of the money so he asked. At her funeral."

"I hope you said no."

"You had to be really naive to believe him. He was that obvious."

"And his parents? Are they around?"

"I think he burned them years ago. I heard or read that they refused to comment on the trial."

I wondered if that meant something. Should I try to find them? Then I asked, "Do you know who Emily Fante is?"

She was quiet for what seemed like a very long time. "Is that going to come up when I testify? I mean, it's just an opportunity to talk about what a good person Madeline is. Isn't that right?"

"So you *do* know who Emily Fante is."

"Madeline would prefer that I not talk about Emily."

That explained why Melody had lied about knowing who Emily was. It wasn't Melody who'd changed her mind, it was Madeline. "Is Emily the woman Wes was having an affair with?"

"No. Absolutely not."

"Do you know who Wes was having an affair with?"

"No. I don't."

"Does Madeline know?"

"I think so. She said a couple of things that gave me that impression. But I can't say for certain."

"I spoke to the office manager at Madeline's old practice. She didn't seem to like Madeline much."

"Cynthia? No, she doesn't like Maddy."

"Do you know why?"

"I do. But Madeline would rather I not talk about it."

"That's part of the history you won't talk about?"

"Yes, it is."

"It's connected then. The reason Madeline's parents won't testify. The anger at the office. Emily Fante. It's all one thing."

"Look, it doesn't have anything to do with what happened with Wes. And it would just make Madeline look bad if it came out."

"Whatever this is...why didn't it come out at the trial?"

"Madeline confessed. After that, I don't think there was much of an investigation."

"Did the police speak to you?"

"A detective came by after my name was put on Madeline's witness list. He only asked what I knew about Wes' affair."

"And you told him what you told me? That Madeline had mentioned it a few times?"

"No. I didn't say that. I said I got that *impression*. Madeline never talked about Wes having an affair. Not until...that day. That's what I told the police."

"I was brought on after the trial. Could you quickly recap your testimony?"

"Very little of it was allowed. Madeline called me that morning. She suspected that Wes was seeing someone else. That was the first time she'd actually come out and said it. She was upset. She planned to confront him that night."

"Did she love him?"

Lana was silent.

"I mean, to get that angry about an affair. She had to have strong feelings for him."

"That's what's so odd. I don't think she did love him. I keep wondering why she didn't just divorce him. None of this makes sense."

I was out of questions so I thanked her for the water and left. The sun was almost entirely gone, allowing the temperature to drop. The rain we'd had earlier was turning into a wet, sloppy snow. In the middle of April. Fortunately, I was just around the corner from Brian's. I turned up my collar, pulled my overcoat tight around me and walked down Lake Shore Drive to Aldine.

When I walked into Brian's apartment I smelled cooking. Terry sat on the couch playing Atari. There was a stack of schoolbooks on the coffee table. I had the feeling that Brian had put them there to remind the boy to eventually do his homework. It was unlikely that Terry would. Brian came out of the kitchen with a glass of wine in one hand.

"What's for dinner?" I asked.

"Fried Chicken, mashed potatoes, hush puppies."

"You're going to town. Special occasion?"

"Actually, Franklin is cooking dinner."

"Oh, he's back."

"He never left," Brian said with a blush.

"Do you want privacy? I can take Terry out to dinner." Although the prospect of slogging through another dinner with the boy didn't appeal.

"No, that's not necessary."

"How did you meet this guy?" I said quietly so it couldn't be heard in the kitchen.

"Big Nell's. I've known him for a while."

"I see."

"Come into the kitchen and have a glass of wine with us."

I followed him through the swinging door into the kitchen. The room was large and square, with new white laminate countertops and sleek cupboards without visible handles. Franklin stood in front of the white electric stove. There were pots on every burner.

"This is Franklin's mother's recipe for fried chicken. His family's originally from Georgia." The implication being that fried chicken there was better. Personally, I'd have been happier having pizza delivered. "Franklin, you remember Nick."

"Yes, I do." Which apparently was supposed to do for hello.

"Nice to see you again," I lied.

"Did you hear that they found the cause of AIDS?" Brian asked, as he handed me a glass of white wine.

"No, I didn't."

"It's an infectious agent. A virus."

"Didn't you already tell me that?"

"I told you they *thought* it might be a virus. Now they know for sure."

"Was that in the newspaper?" I read them pretty religiously and I didn't remember anything about this.

"The report is coming out soon."

"So it's still rumors?"

"They want to close down the bathhouses in San Francisco," Franklin said. "About time if you ask me. I mean, we've known for years that kind of behavior caused it. We didn't have to wait until we knew it was a virus."

"Well, now that they know things will get better," Brian said, upbeat. "I mean, you can't cure something if you don't know what it is."

I almost said, "Like they cured the common cold" but I couldn't. It seemed wrong to be mean to Brian in that particular moment.

"The only smart thing to do is to pair up. Get a boyfriend you can trust and you'll be fine," Franklin said, and threw a smile over his shoulder at Brian. I couldn't help thinking there were all sorts of things wrong with that theory. If a virus caused AIDS, it could easily have traveled from Ross to Brian or from Harker to me to Brian. And those were just the parts of Brian's sex life that I was aware of. As much as I liked Brian, picking him out as a boyfriend didn't seem that much safer than having sex with complete strangers...except, of course, for Brian's new penchant for condoms. Though who really knew if those made a difference.

I could tell from his face that Brian was uncomfortable with the direction the conversation had taken—probably because he was smart enough to think the same things I did—so it wasn't surprising when he changed the subject. "Sugar wants to go to the Glory Hole Saturday night. You should come with us, Nick."

"The Glory Hole?" Franklin said, with acid in his voice. "You didn't say that before. You just said drinks with Sugar Pilson."

"There's a drag queen who does her, Sugar Pills," Brian explained. "Sugar wants to see her. She's been after me forever to take her."

The frown on Franklin's face said that he'd been excited about drinks with Sugar Pilson but had little interest in Sugar Pills. Just to be annoying I picked that moment to say, "Sure I'll go. Sounds fun."

"Why do we always have to be like that?" Franklin asked the air.

"Like what?" Brian wondered.

"Everything's always about the freaks. Whenever they talk about gays on TV or in the movies it's always the leather guys or the drag queens or the guys who fuck everything that moves. Some of us are normal, but you'd never know it by the way we're portrayed." Franklin clucked as he turned the chicken with a pair of tongues. "It just doesn't seem like a good idea to expose someone as important as Sugar Pilson to that kind of element."

"She asked to go," Brian said. Though I could tell he was a bit cowed.

"I think I need a real drink," I said and walked back out to the dining room to pour myself a scotch. Brian's telephone was in the living room. He'd set a comfortable little chair next to the phone stand; after I poured my drink I went and sat down. It was almost eight. Owen Lovejoy, Esquire would probably be at home so I called him there.

While I listened to the phone ring, I said to Terry, "Why don't you turn that off and do your homework?"

"Why don't you mind your own business?"

"In ten years when you're a desperate loser who can't put a roof over his own head I'll remind you that you didn't do your homework."

I don't know what he said to that because Owen picked up the phone. "Hey, there are a couple things I need to talk to you about," I said, not bothering with "hello."

"Okay." He seemed a little distracted and I wondered if I'd caught him walking in the door.

"First, why was there a trial? Why wasn't Madeline offered a deal?"

"They wouldn't do it. I think the ASA is trying to make a name for himself."

I absorbed that and went on. "I talked to Madeline's best friend. There's something going on that she won't talk about. But I did find out that it's all connected. The conflict with her parents. The conflict at her practice. This Emily Fante woman. It's all one thing. You don't know what it is, do you?"

"No, I don't. Could it be something that would help us?" There was a little hint of hope in his voice.

"Lana Shepherd doesn't think so."

"We need to be sure."

"Can you explain that to your client? She's the one who doesn't want people talking about it."

"I have explained it to her."

He sounded a little testy so I said, "Sorry."

"Madeline is a difficult person. Which I suppose isn't uncommon among murderers. Is that all you need?"

"I think so."

"All right. Keep digging around."

He seemed about to hang up so I quickly said, "Um, you wouldn't like a little company." Things had cooled since I'd moved in with Brian. For most of February and March, I could basically just roll over and be fucking, that made me lax about keeping my weekly date with Owen. Since it looked like Brian was now occupied it might not be a bad thing—

"I have company, dear. Thank you for asking, though," he said and then hung up.

As I put the receiver back in the cradle, I realized the living room was quiet. Terry had turned off the Atari and was doing his homework.

Chapter Six

I did know one reason the task force was hot to get Jimmy. Publicity. For about the last four years the FBI had been running an undercover sting called Operation Greylord. Basically they had a lawyer in their pocket who would bribe judges on tape. Once they got one, they got more, and Cook County judges began to fall like dominos. They'd just gotten their first conviction in March, but Operation Greylord had been in the papers for more than a year. Every agent in every agency was chomping at the bit to make a newsworthy bust. They all wanted to be a modern day Elliot Ness. That was half of what Operation Tea and Crumpets was about. It was also why they'd given it a cute, newspaper-ready name.

The murders they were trying to pin on Jimmy took place in 1972. A low-level member of the Outfit named Shady Perelli and his wife, Josette, were found dead in the trunk of their 1971 Cadillac Eldorado. The car had been parked in front of a Sambo's in Downer's Grove for three days. Perelli and his wife were both shot in the back of the head with a small caliber handgun. The murders were professional and there was little in the way of physical evidence. The exact murder scene was never discovered.

The murder weapon was never found. There were no witnesses.

Murders of this sort often went unsolved, and when they were solved they were solved by someone in the Outfit turning State's evidence. So the only thing Operation Tea and Crumpets had going for them was an informant who said Jimmy had ordered the murders and some kind of document that referred to them.

I had just one problem with that.

The most reliable way to solve a murder connected to the Outfit was to look at who benefited. Murders within the Outfit happened when one Outfit guy wanted to take over another Outfit guy's territory, or when one Outfit guy was afraid another Outfit guy was about to go State's evidence. The thing about murdering the Perelli's was that I couldn't see how Jimmy benefited. As nearly as I could tell from the files, Perelli wasn't a threat to Jimmy. And I was pretty sure that in 1972 Jimmy wouldn't have needed to take Perelli's territory. The fact that Jimmy wouldn't have gotten much out of the Perilli murders lent credence to the idea the Feds were attempting to pin the wrong murders on him.

Wednesday I was back in my office ready to work on Jimmy's case. My plan had been to split my days half and half, but that hadn't actually worked out. I'd spent the whole previous day on Madeline Levine and now owed Jimmy some time. It was seven-thirty in the morning. I'd left late enough that I was able to buy a fancy gourmet coffee at The Coffee & Tea Exchange. I got a large, which managed to stay almost hot on the walk over to my office and, unsurprisingly, tasted a whole lot better than the coffee from White Hen. The morning was overcast and cold. It was one of those days where it's humid enough that you wonder if it might be drizzling, and you're not sure until you wind up soaked.

I had a little trouble focusing on Jimmy's case. For one thing, I was hungover. For another, I was annoyed. Even though he seemed to have just shown up in Brian's life, Franklin was taking the kind of ownership that reminded me of someone who'd just gotten the keys to a new car. And worse, he wasn't the friendly sort who wanted to give all his friends rides. No, he was the sort who wanted to keep the car spotless and to himself.

We were just about finished with dinner and I was halfway through my third scotch when I realized he hadn't asked me a single question. In fact, he'd been doing a bang up job of not talking to me at all. He talked to Brian. I talked to Brian. We didn't actually talk to each other.

"We should go to the dunes this summer," Franklin said. I'd heard of them, but never been.

"That sounds like fun," Brian said.

"What about going back to New York?" I asked. "Are you and Sugar planning another trip?"

"We're talking about it."

"New York is a horrible city. Dirty and crime-ridden." Franklin's disapproval had the finality of a door closing.

I'd never had a reason to go to New York so I couldn't defend it. Though I was tempted to anyway. Particularly since you could say the same things about Chicago.

"Franklin works at a law firm in the loop," Brian said as though that explained something. "He's a paralegal."

"I see," I said because I couldn't think of anything else.

"Nick works for a law firm, too. He's an investigator."

"We have an investigator at our firm. I think he's an ex-convict," Franklin said casually. I just smiled at that, though I knew perfectly well the investigator had to be clear of felonies for at least ten years in order to have a license. The point wasn't that their investigator was an ex-con. The point was Franklin didn't like me.

Despite the unpleasantness of the conversation, the dinner was actually good. When I finished I went into the living room and hung out on the sofa, which was basically my "room." Terry had taken his dinner into his bedroom and *Hart to Hart* was on television. The ridiculousness of the show made me giggle a few times. Franklin and Brian cleaned up and I could tell that Franklin was chafed that I wasn't doing the dishes. But even in the living room I could hear him bossing Brian around, and that wouldn't have flown with me so I didn't feel bad. I fell asleep sometime during the local news.

As I took the last sips of my morning coffee, I tried to focus on Jimmy's case. The main thing I needed to do was discover who their informant was. From the transcripts I'd read, the informant knew a great deal about Jimmy. He was close to Jimmy. Close enough to steal or copy some kind of datebook or a series of datebooks, or diary, or journal. Of course, I needed to sit down with Jimmy and ask him about that, but it seemed a good idea to make a little progress first. I wanted to study the files I'd put together and read through everything again, but I didn't think that would yield much. I knew what I needed to do; I just didn't want to do it. I finished off the coffee, tossed the Styrofoam cup into my trash basket, and pulled my overcoat back on. It was time to go down to the Loop.

Operation Tea and Crumpets was working out of the Federal Building on Dearborn. From the information in the files, I knew that the interviews were taking place in their office on the twenty-third floor. What I wanted to know was who went in and out of the building, but even before I went down, I knew that was going to be difficult. I took the Jackson/Howard down to Jackson, and when I climbed up out of the subway I was right at the Federal building plaza staring at the big red bird by Calder.

The Federal Building was a black monolith by Mies van der Rohe of forty-some floors; across the street was the Courthouse, another van der Rohe building of only thirty floors, though much wider. Just beyond the Calder was a mammoth, one-story Post Office made of the same black metal used in the other two buildings. I was looking for someplace to watch the lobby of the federal building. My options were limited.

I circled the building. Across Jackson was a hundred-year-old, sixteen-story brick building. I eyed it seriously for a few minutes. If I could rent an office on the second floor then I'd be able to watch the entrance to the Federal Building. But that was a big if. Even if an office was available, I had no way of knowing if the landlord would go for something short term. And, if they somehow learned that I was watching the Federal Building in order to keep tabs on a Federal investigation, they might not feel too comfortable. I considered the Post Office for a moment. Like most Post Offices there were long lines most of the day. I could slip from long line to long line, keeping my eye on the Federal Building the whole time. But I figured sooner or later someone would notice me hanging around and ask me to buy some stamps or get out.

Walking into the lobby of the Federal Building I quickly saw that there were even fewer possibilities in there. In fact, there barely was an "in there." The lobby, enclosed in two-story glass windows, was nothing but a shiny floor, some pillars, and a few elevator banks. The back of the elevator bank was an expanse of tile with the Federal Seal in the middle.

Dozens of people walked across the lobby, on their way to offices upstairs, on their way out of the building. I wondered how many thousands of people walked across the space every day. There was no place to go unnoticed, though. Everyone was visible and anyone standing around for hours would draw attention. On the wall by the elevators was a directory. I studied it for a few minutes. There was no listing for anything on the twenty-third floor. The IRS was on the twenty-fourth, and on the twenty-second the office of Alderman Kenkowski of the Second Ward.

Without thinking too much about it, I got into one of the elevators and pressed 23. The elevator filled and began to rise. The first stop was the twentieth floor. Another elevator ran from the first floor to the nineteenth. The second stop was twenty-three and I got off. Luckily, I got off alone and found myself in a cream-colored space with doors at either end. I walked to my right and looked up and down the bland hallway. Most of the office spaces were just labeled with numbers. There was a law office at the end of the hallway, Clarkson and Peters, which I guessed did a lot of business with the Federal government. Halfway down was a men's room. I tried the door but it was locked and required a key. It didn't matter. I couldn't hang out in the restroom all day. Not only would it be suspicious if anyone noticed me but there was no guarantee I'd learn anything.

I walked by the elevator and entered the other hallway. It was virtually indistinguishable from the first. Most of the offices were again unmarked. I tried a couple of the doors, ready to tell anyone inside that I was looking for Clarkson and Peters, but the doors were locked. Near the end of the hallway, I found an office with a plaque that said "British Export Company." *Clever*, I thought. Most people wouldn't think twice about their business name. Even though if there were a real British Export Company they'd be located in England. A company doing similar business in the United States would be called British Import Company.

Letting my hand rest on the doorknob, I tried to think whether to try to open it. It would be interesting to see their setup. If anyone was in there I could say I was looking for the attorney's office like I'd planned, even though that would make me look like I couldn't read a plaque on the door. The thing is, worse than looking stupid, I was afraid of being recognized. It wasn't likely but I might know whoever they had from the CPD. Or, I might be recognized later on…I wasn't sure I should risk it. I wasn't even sure I knew what it was I wanted to see. I took my hand off the door and walked back down the hallway to the elevator. Pushing the down button, I stood there waiting.

Then I heard a door open far down the hallway I'd just come from. I pushed the down button again, even though I knew perfectly well the elevator wouldn't come any faster. Voices grew closer as I waited. I considered running around the corner into the other hallway but that seemed ridiculous. I didn't even know if the voices coming down the hall were part of the task force. There were other doors they could have come out of. On top of that, if they were from the task force, an elevator mysteriously opening with no one there might raise—

The elevator opened, I stepped into the car. I hit the down button a number of times hoping that the door would close before the voices got there. But it didn't. Two men in their late thirties got into the car. They were both thick-bodied, kept their hair in crew cuts, and wore inexpensive suits with trench coats draped over their arms. In my experience, they looked like Federal agents. I looked like a bum who'd lost his way.

Quickly, I reached over and hit 22 before the doors closed, by way explanation I said, "Wrong floor. Did you know if you actually come down and complain to your Alderman about potholes they fix them? We got this pothole so deep you can see the cobblestone down underneath it."

One of them said, "No kidding."

"It works better to come down. If you just call or write a letter they only fix it half the time. Showing up it's a hundred percent. Guess they're afraid you'll come back."

The door opened and we were at the twenty-second floor. I got off and looked around as though I was actually trying to find my Alderman's office. The door closed behind me and I stopped. I decided I needed to wait at least ten minutes before I went down to the lobby. If the agents were at all suspicious they'd wait down there to see how long I took. There was an ashtray on the wall between the elevator banks; I lit up a cigarette and considered my situation. I needed to know who was coming in and out of the task force's offices. It was the best way to determine who their informant was. But there was no easy way to set up surveillance. There was no hard way that I could see either.

By the time I finished my cigarette I decided to head back to my office and go through the boxes again. There had to be something in there that would lead me to the informant. But even as I rode the elevator down and walked back across the lobby and out to the subway, I began to wonder if there wasn't another way to approach this.

I went back over the basics. Shady and Josette Perelli had been murdered, or rather, hit. Murder is a word that implies some level of passion. They were hit. Taken out of existence for purely business reasons. According to Prince Charles, a soldier named Nino "The Nose" Nitti killed the couple on Jimmy's orders. Nitti died seven years after the Perellis in 1979. He was shanked in a prison shower. He was about to be paroled, early and somewhat suspiciously. What Nitti was in prison for was not mentioned in the files. I had no idea if it was relevant.

The El train's doors opened and let me out at the Belmont stop. I'd been riding in one of the old green cars with the stiff leather seats. One of the windows didn't close all the way so it had been a chilly ride. Still, I liked that it had kept me awake and thinking. It seemed like a good idea to find someone who knew The Nose. I sat down on one of the wooden benches that dot the platform. I was trying to decide if I should cross over to the other side of the platform and head back to the library and do some research on The Nose. There had to be newspaper stories about him. His arrests. His death. What I needed were relatives. A wife. Kids. Someone he might have confessed to. They wouldn't be in the articles necessarily, but his address would. It would give me a place to start. I decided I'd start there in the morning. I didn't feel like trekking back downtown.

I walked down the wooden stairs into the station, which had to be seventy or eighty years old and looked every day of it. The electric blue paint was thick and heavily chipped. The wooden steps sagged in the middle where foot traffic had worn them down. The ticket taker's booth, only a bit bigger than a phone booth, was original, but the silver turnstiles were not. In fact, much of the station probably was not. I imagined the wood being replaced over and over again as the weather and millions of feet wore it down. I went through the tall turnstile that led to the street.

In front of the station, a woman in a white uniform held a plastic bucket collecting coins as people walked by. I wasn't sure if she was Salvation Army or not. They usually only came out at Christmas. But it was nearly Easter, maybe that's why they were reappearing. I started down Belmont toward Clark, but then I stopped and turned to look at the woman again. She'd given me an idea, an idea that might actually work.

Chapter Seven

I was hungry when I walked into my office. I wondered if I should buy one of those little fridges and stock it with snacks. Or at least ice cubes. It would be nice to sit at my desk and have a scotch on the rocks once and a while. Of course, I could simply walk over to Brian's and rifle through his kitchen for a sandwich or something, but I was beginning to feel like I'd accepted enough of his hospitality. Which didn't mean I was going to run out and get the *Reader* to start looking for an apartment. It just meant I needed to start thinking about doing something.

My answering machine had five messages. I felt popular. I ran the tape back so I could hear them. The first message was from Mrs. Harker, my sort of onetime mother-in-law. All she said was, "Is Easter Sunday, you come to dinner." Which meant that I was to show up at her condo in Edison Park at two o'clock Sunday afternoon, preferably shaved, showered, and wearing a pressed shirt. I'd been to dinner a number of times that winter, but that had stopped when Mrs. Harker found out that her priest had lied to her about the departure of the deacon, who'd been having sex with his students, including Terry. Father Dewes had told her the Deacon was dismissed due to theft. She hadn't appreciated being lied to and somehow her priest lying to her became my fault. Apparently, though, she'd forgiven me, so now I had to go out and have some ham to celebrate Christ's resurrection.

The second message was a woman saying, "Hello? Is someone there?" I didn't recognize the voice. She said, "Hello" a couple more times and then hung up with a clunk. I rewound the tape and listened again. She didn't sound happy. But then, she might have been calling to sell me something. Something she wasn't happy about.

The third message was Joseph, "Hi. I'm calling to confirm dinner tomorrow and to give you my number. I realized you didn't have it and I thought if you had to cancel you wouldn't be able to reach me. I don't want you to cancel, don't get that idea. I just thought, you know, you should be able to reschedule if something came up." I scrambled for a piece of paper as he gave me the number. As I wrote it down, I was happy. Too happy. And that bothered me. Though I couldn't figure out if it was because he was a priest; going on a date with a priest couldn't possibly be a good idea. Or was I bothered because I wasn't ready to be happy in that way? I didn't know. Wasn't sure I wanted to know. Maybe I should just be happy and not worry about it.

The next message started and I was barely paying attention. "This is Kimmy Crete. I heard through the grapevine that you wanted to talk to me. I called Maddy's lawyer and got your number. Um, I'm available whenever. I'm not working so, just give me a call if you want to talk about something. I really want to help Maddy. She was always nice to me."

The final message was silence. I had the feeling it was the same woman who'd called earlier but there was no way to tell. Now I had a decision to make. I was hungry and wanted to go have lunch, but I also wanted to return Joseph's call and possibly Kimmy's.

I dialed Joseph first. When he answered I said, "I didn't think you had a phone. I was imagining you living like a monk in a barren room with a twin bed and a crucifix on the wall."

"You're not that far off. But I do have a phone all to myself. We're medieval but still civilized. I'm glad you called me back."

"You may not be that glad in a minute."

"You're going to cancel, aren't you?"

"Actually, I'm wondering if we could have dinner tonight and see a movie if you'd like."

"I'm supposed to have a counseling session at six. I could be at your office at seven-thirty. Is that too late?"

"No, it's fine. I need a favor though."

"All right."

"Could you bring one of your black suits with the black shirt and clerical collar?" I asked as blandly as I could.

"Um…we should stick to dinner and a movie. And even if we weren't I don't think I'd want—"

"No. I'm not going to ask you to wear it while we…it's for me—"

"That's not any better."

"It's for me to wear to work."

"Are you changing professions?"

"I need to watch a building downtown. I'm going to get a bucket, wear your suit, and collect money for Easter Seals or something. That way I can watch everyone who's going in and out and not be suspicious."

"Oh. Well, all right. I'd be more comfortable if you promise not to perform any sacraments."

"I'm not planning any."

"And the money you raise?"

"Can go to the charity of your choice."

I thanked him in advance and told him I was looking forward to our evening, then hung up. My stomach gurgled, but I decided to make a quick call to Kimmy Crete before heading out to find some lunch. She answered quickly and agreed to meet with me at her apartment in about a half an hour. She lived on Lincoln Park West near the zoo. After I hung up, I hurried out of my office. I walked down Clark to Belmont and found a greasy gyros place I liked. I got a gyros wrapped in foil and a bag of French fries. I scarfed them down as quickly as I could, swallowed a sixteen ounce Coke in a few gulps, and was back on the street a few minutes later hailing a cab for the nine block ride. I could have waited for a 22 bus but didn't have the patience.

The cab let me off right in front of 2020 Lincoln Park West. The building was about forty-stories, cement, with half-circle balconies going all the way to the top. The doorman announced me and I was sent to the twenty-seventh floor. I found Kimmy's apartment, 27G, and knocked. A young girl, short and a little on the pudgy side, opened the door. She had perky blond hair that probably cost a fortune to keep up and wore a pair of white flannel pajamas with hearts.

The apartment was a studio. A small bathroom to the right as I walked in, then an equally small kitchen, and a large room that had sliding glass doors as one wall. They led out onto one of the half-circle balconies, which looked cold, damp and uninviting. The place was far too expensive for a dental assistant and even more out of reach for an unemployed dental assistant. I assumed there were a couple of parents in the background despairing of the fact that their daughter hadn't yet found a man to take care of her. The furniture was nice, comfortable. Her pullout bed was still pulled out and a large TV in an entertainment center played an afternoon soap, I think it was *Ryan's Hope* but I'm hardly an expert.

We sat down at a small glass dining table with delicate metal chairs. She offered me tea but I turned it down, hoping I didn't smell too much like onions and grease.

"I only have a few questions. You were a dental hygienist at Caspian Dental Group?"

"No."

"No?"

She shook her head.

I thought for a moment and said, "Oh, sorry, you were a dental hygienist at Caspian Levine Dental Care?"

"Well, yeah, that's right but I wasn't a dental hygienist. I was a dental assistant."

"What's the difference?"

She looked at me like I was stupid. "A dental assistant assists the dentist. A dental hygienist cleans teeth."

"Why did you stop working as a dental assistant at Caspian Dental Group?"

"I was fired."

"Oh? Why were you fired?"

"Math," she said simply.

"I didn't think there was a lot of math involved in being a dental assistant."

"I know, right? But there is. I had to keep track of Dr. Caspian's drugs. You know, he does oral surgery and stuff. So he's got all these painkillers and he's even got pharmaceutical cocaine in there. I guess if you're high enough you don't care what he does to your mouth."

"So you kept inventory."

"I did, yeah."

"And drugs went missing?" I speculated.

"Not missing, exactly. Unaccounted for. Because I can't do math. Nobody there would steal drugs."

"And that's why you were fired. Because the drugs were unaccounted for?"

"Yeah...Dr. Levine-Berkson tried to keep me, but it's all sort of regulated so they had to make someone responsible. Since I can't do math and it was probably all my fault anyway..."

"When I called over there I got the impression that Dr. Levine-Berkson wasn't well liked."

"Cynthia hates her, I know. I could never figure that out. But then I was only there for nine months. They told me Dr. Levine-Berkson was difficult to work with, but she was always really nice to me."

Her attention drifted over to her soap opera. I stared at her and wondered if she was as dense as she seemed. It was very likely that someone was stealing drugs, possibly counting on Kimmy's poor math skills while doing it. Did this girl really not understand that?

Abruptly, she said, "When I got fired, she wrote me a check for five hundred dollars out of her own account."

"Dr. Levine-Berkson did that?"

"Yes.

"Why do you think she did that?"

"Because she's nice."

"She felt bad about your being fired."

"Yeah. A nice person would feel bad, wouldn't they?"

But did she feel bad or did she feel guilty? I wondered. Someone stole drugs but never got caught. Was it Madeline? It would explain Cynthia's cryptic comment about the doctor's personal problems. It would also explain why she felt guilty enough to write a personal check to a girl who was clearly in no danger of starving.

"Wait a minute. Were you the only one who had access to the drugs?"

"No. That would be stupid. They're in a glass case. I had a key and so did both doctors."

"And that's it. Just the three of you?"

"No. Cynthia had a key at the desk. In case I was out. She could give it to a temp."

"So how did it work?"

"Well one of the dentists would ask for something and I'd go get it."

"And you wrote down everything you took."

She shrugged. "I thought I did. But I guess it was only some of the time. Every night I had to make sure everything matched."

"And did it match?"

"No, it never matched."

"Never?"

"No. I knew I was just making mistakes so I kind of fudged the numbers."

"But the dentists or Cynthia could have taken drugs out of the cabinet and not written it down."

"They wouldn't do that."

"How do you know that?"

"God, you're just like my father. He's suspicious of everyone. He doesn't believe I could do anything wrong."

I smiled at her. I got the feeling she didn't believe she could do anything right. She started watching her soap again. I pulled her attention back with, "Do you know anything about a woman named Emily Fante?"

"Mmm-hmmm. Dr. Levine-Berkson had a friend named Emily who used to call. I think she came by once so they could go to lunch."

"Do you remember what she looked like?"

"Older, short hair, almost kind of dyke-y." She blushed when she said the word dyke. As though it was embarrassing that lesbians existed. "It was always weird."

"Because they didn't look like they'd know each other?"

"Yes! That's why it was weird. I mean, I knew it was weird I just didn't know why. Thank you."

"That's all you know about her?"

"Yes. That's all."

"Did Dr. Levine-Berkson ever talk about her family with you? They refuse to testify on her behalf."

"She didn't talk much about them. I mean, I know that her mother took care of her kids for her. Not that it was all that convenient. She had to drive the kids from Skokie to Park Ridge and then come into the city to the practice. Usually it took her an hour in the morning. Longer in the afternoon."

"Did Dr. Levine-Berkson ever talk about her marriage?"

"Well, no. Not to me."

"To someone else?"

"Um. Well, she didn't always take her husband's calls. I mean, even when she wasn't with a patient. And then…" She made me wait, so I did. "One time I overheard her fighting with him on the phone. I mean, I think it was him. She kept saying stuff about how he stole from her. That she gave him an allowance and that should be enough."

"She couldn't have been talking to one of her kids?"

"Oh my God! They're not even in grade school. You don't talk that way to kids. I mean, she was cursing and everything."

"Can you think of anything else that might be helpful?"

"Is this what I have to talk about in court? The lawyer said I just had to talk about how much I liked Dr. Levine-Berkson."

"He's right. You should be honest, but don't volunteer any of this unless they ask you directly."

"Then why do you need to know?"

"I'm looking for something that might help Madeline." But so far I was only finding things that would hurt her. Which made me think of something I should at least ask. "You don't have any idea who Wes Berkson was having an affair with?"

"Maybe. When they were fighting on the phone Dr. Levine-Berkson kept saying Jane. It was all Jane's fault."

"When was this phone call?"

"A week or so before I got fired," she said.

"When did you get fired?"

"I guess it was a year, more than that, fourteen months."

I did some calculations in my head. "You got fired a couple weeks before Dr. Levine-Berkson killed her husband."

"Yeah. I was so surprised. I felt so bad for her. I wish I'd never cashed her check."

"So, the conversation you're talking about when she and her husband fought over money and someone named Jane was about a month before she killed her husband."

"Yes. I guess."

I thanked her and stood up to leave.

"Oh, that's it?"

"Yes, thank you for your help."

She walked me to the door. It wasn't a long walk. As she opened the door for me, she said, "You know I'm still looking for a job. Do you need anybody? I mean, your job looks really easy."

Chapter Eight

I was a good boy and took the 22 back to my office. My head was spinning. If Madeline was fighting with her husband about his girlfriend a month before she killed him then her story was a fabrication. She didn't stab him because he suddenly admitted the affair. She already knew about it. And, she claimed not to know who he was having an affair with. But, if this Jane person was actually the woman Wes was seeing then Madeline did know, or very least knew the woman's first name and had a month to find out more. Not to mention, a month to get angry enough to stab her husband.

Or, she might have stabbed him for another reason. A reason she didn't want people to know. I remembered the comment Melody made about her sister. That she'd lie to make herself look better. Was she doing that? Was there something worse than being a jilted wife going on here?

And the missing drugs. What did that mean? I'd already confirmed with Lana that the anger at the office, Madeline's distant parents, and the mysterious Emily Fante were all connected. So, was the connection drugs? Drugs would explain the anger at the office—especially if it was Madeline who was stealing the drugs and letting Kimmy take the fall. It would also explain the problems with her family. But how does it explain Emily Fante? Was she Madeline's drug dealer? And how did it all connect to her husband spending too much money and having a girlfriend?

When I got back to the office there was another hang up on my machine. It seemed clear that someone wanted to talk to me but didn't want to leave a message. It was almost two o'clock and I didn't have anything planned for the afternoon until seven-thirty, when Joseph was coming by. I wanted to crawl up on the sofa and take a nap. It was a heck of a lot more comfortable that the one I was sleeping on at Brian's. My neck could use the change of scenery. But I decided not to. What I really needed to do was find a relative of The Nose and nose around a little. I laughed at my little pun and realized, not for the first time, that I was a little too good at being alone. Focus, I told myself. Should I go downtown to the library and do a newspaper search? Or maybe go visit Harker's old partner, Detective Frank Connors. He might know something about The Nose. He'd been around long enough.

Then I had a realization. There might be information on The Nose right in front of me. The whole reason I knew The Nose was implicated in the Perelli murders was that I'd read it in a transcript of an interview with Prince Charles. I had fifteen boxes of information. I'd organized it all. Read most, but not all of it. There were about thirty-two different files on known associates of Jimmy English. These included members of a crew he oversaw; the management of Lucky Days, a small casino he owned part of in Las Vegas—which seemed at least partly legit; and various lowlifes who were believed to have done jobs for him.

I'd organized and relabeled everything, so it wasn't that hard to find the box containing known associates. There was a file on The Nose. It was thin, but still a file. I opened it. Inside were a page of notes referencing both the transcript of a conversation with Prince Charles, which I had, and page numbers for the diary or journal or whatever that I didn't have. After that was an arrest record which included The Nose's last known address. That was someplace to start.

I pulled the Greater Chicago Metropolitan Phonebook out of a drawer. Mine was from 1981. I also had a couple of suburban phonebooks, so I took out the Oak Park Forest Park River Forest phonebook from 1983 to go along with it. The Nose's last known address was in Forest Park. Forest Park was a step down from Oak Park but still had some nice parts. For some reason these gangster types liked the ritzy western suburbs. Jimmy lived in Oak Park.

I checked the Metropolitan phonebook first and found that The Nose still lived at the same address. Well, he didn't live there; he'd been dead for two years by then. But in 1981 there was still a phone listed in his name. Widows did that. They left a phone in their husband's name so that people didn't make obscene phone calls. It was strange that more people didn't unlist their phone numbers. Yeah, the phone company charged about a buck a month to *not* list your number, which didn't make a whole lot of sense. But if people realized how easy it was to find them and find out things about them, they'd probably pony up the money. Then I checked the Oak Park Forest Park River Forest phonebook and found that Nino Nitti still had a phone at the same address on Thatcher in Forest Park. I had five hours. If I walked over to Aldine and found my car I could be out in Forest Park in about forty minutes. I grabbed my overcoat and was out of the office in two.

It took three tries to get the car started—I hadn't used it in a while—and then I had to find a gas station. I made the mistake of filling up the tank, which set me back nearly thirty bucks. For a small car, the Nova has a big tank and gas prices in the city are larcenous. Nearly a buck and half. Since I'd divested myself of all my cash, I had to stop at a Cash Station and pull out thirty bucks for my date with Joseph. I could have done that later, but I had the feeling I was on my way to torture an old lady. When I realized why I was stalling, I promised myself I'd be nice no matter what and got on the road.

The Nitti house looked like something out of *Leave It to Beaver*. A two story, clapboard with a New England feel, it was yellow with white trim. It looked like the kind of house where only happy things happened. There was not a single thing about it that said it had been purchased, at least in part, by money made killing people. Across the street was a thickly wooded area. The trees and grass were struggling to come back to life, but tentatively, since even the plants knew we sometimes got snow in April—as we had two days before. It crossed my mind that those woods were a great place to dump a body. As I walked up to the house I wondered if any of The Nose's handiwork was buried across the street from his house.

I rang the doorbell and waited. I thought I might have to wait awhile. If I remembered The Nose's arrest record correctly, he had been in his early sixties when he died five years before. That meant his widow had to be around retirement age. I didn't expect she'd be moving quickly. But then the door was opened abruptly by a man of about my age. He was bland-looking and a little pudgy around the middle. I started to tell him who I was, but he interrupted me. "You're a cop. You think I can't tell a cop when I see one."

Still? was my first thought. My second was that I should play this honest. "I used to be a cop. Now I'm a private investigator. My name is Nick Nowak and I'm doing some work for Jimmy English."

He laughed. "A cop and a gangster. Welcome to Chicago."

"I'm getting the impression you're pissed off. You want to tell me why?"

He looked at me suspiciously. I didn't think he was expecting a friendly response. "Cops were out here. They wanted to talk to my mother. Wanted her to say that she remembered dad talking about killing the Perelli's for Jimmy."

"And does she remember that?"

"My mother's got early senility. She can't remember how to feed herself."

"I'm sorry about that. It sounds terrible."

"Thank you," he said grudgingly. "So you work for Jimmy English?"

"Yeah."

"Here's the thing. When they found out about my mom they put all sorts of pressure on me. They wanted me to say I remembered my father talking about those murders."

"But he never talked about them?"

"He never talked about any of that. He kept us separate. Look, I'm a CPA and I live in Indianapolis. The only mob guy I ever met was my own dad. He was proud of that. He would rather die than talk to me about the shit he did."

I took one of my cards out of my pocket and wrote down the number for Cooke, Babcock and Lackerby, and Owen's name.

"What's your name?"

"Same as my dad's." I hoped he meant he was Nino, Jr. and not The Nose, Jr.

"Nino, this is the name of Jimmy's attorney. If anyone—"

"I don't want to be involved. I'm putting the house on the market. Moving Mom to a nursing home in Mooresville. I'm done with Chicago."

"All right. Take the card though. If they come back again Jimmy's attorney will stop them harassing you. Okay?"

Reluctantly, he took the card from me and then, without a goodbye, shut the door. I walked back to the car slowly. It was barely three. I had plenty of time. And I was near Oak Park. *I should go see Jimmy*, I thought. I had questions I needed answered. But I also knew I probably shouldn't show up on his doorstep. Even if he was okay with it, I doubted that Owen Lovejoy, Esquire would appreciate my going without his knowledge. Still, I had the time and a full tank of gas and it was a short drive east to Oak Park.

Jimmy's house looked the same as it had on my two previous visits. It was a two-story brick colonial. The shrubs in front were evergreen and looked good even in the dank gray of early spring. There was a black Sedan DeVille sitting in the driveway. That was not the same. It was brand new. Every time I visited there was a new Cadillac in the driveway.

I parked on the street rather than in the driveway. Even though Jimmy had given me the car I wasn't sure he'd want it seen in his driveway. Electric green with black stripes and mag wheels, it was an eyesore and sooner or later I needed to get rid of it. When I got to the front door, I rang the bell. It only took a few moments for a black maid with a Jamaican accent to answer. She was new, but she was just as haughty as the last maid. After giving her my name, I told her I wanted to see Jimmy and that he wasn't expecting me. If he didn't have time to see me I understood. She looked me up and down, and left me where I was, closing the door nearly shut.

It took a long time for her to come back and I was afraid he wouldn't see me. I was a little nervous. Jimmy had been kind to me and had shown a great deal of generosity when I'd done work for him, but he was still part of the Outfit. I had a pretty good idea of what he was capable of if you got on the wrong side of him. Finally, the maid came back. With a sniff and her nose in the air, she led me through the house, through the kitchen, to a door that led to the basement.

In the basement, Jimmy had built a full bar complete with red leather stools and a dartboard. I expected to find him behind the bar waiting for me, but the basement was empty. I sat on one of the stools and wondered if it would be okay to have a cigarette. There was a glass ashtray on the bar that had a matchbook inside of it that was embossed with the words, "Jimmy's Place." I decided to take that as an invitation to light up. I was two drags in when Jimmy came down the stairs. Slowly. He looked as though he'd aged quite a lot. I wondered if he was eighty now. He'd lost weight and there was a curve in his back that I didn't remember. When he reached the bottom of the stairs he looked up at me with a certain curiosity.

"I was in the neighborhood, Jimmy. I hope you don't mind me stopping by."

"Should I mind? Are you bringing trouble?"

"I'm bringing questions. You know I'm working with your attorneys."

"I know that. I still pay my own bills."

"Thank you if you had anything to do with my—"

"Do you want a drink?"

"Sure. Do you want me to get—"

"I like to do it."

He walked slowly around the bar, picked out a rocks glass, and filled it with ice from a small ice machine. I wondered if the maid came down every so often to dump out some of the ice in order to keep it fresh. Without asking he poured me a Johnnie Walker Red. He slid it in front of me on a cocktail napkin. Then poured himself a Coke from a soda gun.

Abruptly, he said, "My wife passed away last year."

"I'm sorry Jimmy. I didn't know. Last year was kind of rough on me. I wasn't paying a lot of attention."

"Yes, I know."

I wasn't sure whether he meant he knew I'd had a bad year or if he was saying he'd had a bad year, too. I wasn't sure if it mattered. I took out and a pen and wrote on the cocktail napkin he'd given me. IS IT SAFE TO TALK?

"I have a guy. He comes in and waves this little transistor radio thing around. It's like magic. He says we're okay."

"So, you know I'm going through the materials I was given."

He nodded.

"There are notations, page numbers and comments that seem to refer to a journal or a diary. Did you keep any kind of records like that?" The question made me nervous. Basically, I was asking, "So, Jimmy every time you broke the law were you stupid enough to write it down?"

Fortunately, he didn't take it that way. He just shook his head.

"Was there anyone close to you who might have…written things down?"

"No. No, I trust my people."

"The notes cover a very long period of time. It would have to be someone who has known you a long time."

He nodded, but that seemed to make no difference.

"They're focusing on the Perelli murders. Can you think of any reason why they'd choose those murders?" I didn't want to ask him outright if he ordered them killed, first because it was a little insulting and second because after my visit to the Nitti house I was convinced he didn't have anything to do with the murders.

He thought for a moment. "Nobody knows much about the Perelli murders. We could say Harold Washington did it and if we got an all-white jury he'd go to jail." The reference to our new mayor made me laugh. It was true, though. The evidence in the Perelli murders was so scant that even the appearance of evidence could get Jimmy convicted with the right jury.

"What was Shady Perelli like?"

"A loudmouth. Liked to brag. His wife was worse."

"Those aren't good qualities to have in your business."

"No, they get you killed."

"You know who ordered them killed, don't you?" I could feel my pulse beating in my throat when I asked that.

"I didn't order the hit."

"I don't think you did. But you do know who did."

He frowned at me. "I can't tell you that."

"Why not? You said the room isn't bugged."

"It's not safe for you to know everything."

A chill crept up the back of my neck and I nearly shook. But he'd told me what I needed to know. The order for the Perelli hit had come from someone above him. Someone who wouldn't like my knowing about their involvement."

"The task force thinks that The Nose did the actual hit."

"That's the rumor."

"I went to see The Nose's widow. The task force had been there wanting her to say that The Nose confessed to her that you're the one who ordered the hit on the Perellis."

"Is she going to do that?"

"No. She's senile, can't remember much of anything. So they tried to get the son to say the same thing. He refused."

Jimmy nodded again. "They don't have anything if they're trying to convince people to say things they don't want to say."

"All they have is their informant. They call him Prince Charles."

Jimmy chuckled.

"According to Prince Charles you wanted Shady Perelli dead because of a border dispute. He was putting the squeeze on some restaurants that you...provided services to." It's not necessarily a good idea to call extortion by its right name when you're talking to the extortionist.

"That's not true. What is true is that I got some of Shady's territory after he died. A couple people did. It didn't just come to me."

My scotch was almost finished. Jimmy poured me another without asking. I took a deep breath before I said the next. "Jimmy, there's something I want...a promise. If I find Prince Charles nothing bad will happen to him."

"Tell me what you mean by bad?"

"He won't end up dead. If your lawyers know who he is they can find a way to shut him down." I may have been over-estimating Owen Lovejoy, Esquire's abilities.

"Can I be persuasive?"

I was asking a leopard to change his spots and I knew it. Beyond that I knew that the Feds were being pretty persuasive on their own. "You can be as persuasive as you want to be. As long as Prince Charles keeps all his body parts."

That made Jimmy laugh. "You're an interesting young man."

"Thank you."

"I'm not sure I meant it as a compliment." That was meant to chastise me. And it did. We were silent for an uncomfortably long time.

"You know, I'm not sure I have any questions left, Jimmy."

"Then we'll talk like old friends for a minute."

"All right. You'll keep thinking about the diary?" I reminded.

"I'll think about the diary."

I had no idea how to talk to him like a friend. Was I supposed to ask about his family? I'd only met a few of his relatives, one was in prison, another was a sociopathic actress, and the third was a coed with a penchant for middle-aged mobsters. I wasn't comfortable inquiring after any of them.

"Who do you share your secrets with, Jimmy?" It felt like an intimate question but I had to ask it. And now we were old friends.

"My priest. Well, the one I liked died. I don't say too much to the new one. He's too young to know that old men don't change."

"And that's it? Confession?"

"The people above me. They know certain things."

That wasn't helpful. It wasn't how these Federal investigations worked. The task force had to turn someone on the bottom to get to the people on top. You didn't turn the people on top to get to the ones on the bottom. It seemed too much of a stretch to think that Jimmy's bosses had turned on him. In fact, part of the reason to go after someone like Jimmy was to see if he'd turn on his bosses.

"When you reach the end of your life you start to think about what it all meant," Jimmy said. "It's important that it meant something. The thing that matters most in life is family. When it's all over that's what you have. Family."

I smiled weakly. If family was the thing that mattered I was screwed. Mine didn't speak to me. Not that it bothered me much. It had been like that for a long time. I spent a lot more time worrying about my friends than giving thought to my relatives.

Still, it seemed like a good idea to say, "Family's important. Very important."

Chapter Nine

I was back in my office by five-thirty taking notes on both meetings and strategizing on how I might tell Owen Lovejoy, Esquire I'd talked to his client without informing him first. It was unfortunate that I'd let our regular thing slide or that he'd replaced me—whichever had actually happened, I'd barely paid enough attention to be sure. Fucking him would have come in handy at that moment. He was much more likely to accept that I'd gone ahead and spoken to Jimmy on my own if I told him about it while I had my dick up his ass.

But the visit had been worth it. I needed to be certain that Jimmy hadn't kept the journal or diary himself. I believed him when he said he hadn't. That left me thinking that Prince Charles had been the one writing things down. At the very least, he was connected to whoever had written it. If I figured out who he was, I could figure out what he had that was written down. Conversely, if I figured out exactly what the journal/diary was, then that could lead me to Prince Charles. I had a chicken and egg problem and no clue how to find the henhouse.

There were two hang-ups on my answering machine. I figured it was the woman who called earlier. She kept calling, so I had to assume she'd actually talk to me if I picked up the phone. So, why wouldn't she leave a number? Without even thinking about it, I found myself crawling onto the sofa for nap. I tried to put together a plan for the next few days. I was going to spend them in the lobby of the Federal Building collecting for charity. I wondered if I should invest in one of those crazy little cameras they always showed in spy movies. That way I could take pictures of people as they came and went without being noticed. I realized it was actually a good thing I'd been in an elevator with those two Federal agents. If one of them walked in with Prince Charles I might have chance of figuring it out. Otherwise, I realized that the informant could walk by me twenty times a day and I probably wouldn't know it. Staking out the Federal Building was a long shot but at the moment it was the only shot I had of any kind.

I was nearly asleep when the phone rang. Springing up from the couch I grabbed the receiver expecting to find some strange woman on the other end. Unfortunately, it was Frank Connors, Harker's former partner.

"This is unexpected," I said.

"I got a call about you."

"Really, who from?"

"Someone who's looking into you."

"Why would someone look into me?"

"You got a new job, didn't you?"

"Yes. Is that a problem?"

"It seems to be, yes. You're working on something that is pissing people off."

"It's not the first time. It probably won't be the last."

"They're nosing around things I'd rather they didn't nose around." That was a problem. The night I drowned the Bughouse Slasher in the pond at Graceland Cemetery I'd dropped my gun and couldn't find it. Connors had brought it back to me three days later. That meant other people might know about the gun. Connors had probably run the serial number to find out it was mine. If someone was looking into me that meant they could hurt Connors. They could hurt him bad.

"Okay, I'm working on a couple of things. So what exactly is pissing people off?"

"Jimmy English. You're on the wrong side of things, Nick."

I was also helping a murderer get a lighter sentence. It had become my job to be on the wrong side of things. "Look I'm going to tell you a couple of things I shouldn't. They're not playing by the book. They're trying to hang something on Jimmy that he didn't do."

"And you know this because?"

"Because this afternoon I talked to someone they want to use as a witness. Someone they want to feed testimony to."

"I can't worry about that. If I did everything by the book I wouldn't be on the phone with you, would I? Sometimes doing the wrong thing is the right thing. You know that Nick."

"Trying to get people to lie so they can put an old man in prison. That doesn't feel like the right thing."

"He's not an innocent man."

"I know that. But I think they missed their shot."

"Maybe, maybe not. All I know is I don't want to go down to save Jimmy English. And neither do you." He hung up without saying goodbye.

That complicated things. I'd been enjoying the fact that I had a decent paying job that looked like it might go on for a while. The fact that it could put me in prison didn't make me happy. I tried calling Owen, but I got the answering service. I glanced at my clock radio and saw that it was twenty after seven. I must have actually fallen asleep without realizing it.

Joseph was going to be there in a few minutes and I needed to put all of this out of my mind. I wasn't sure I could do that. If he were coming by for a quick fuck I'd be a lot better at putting my thoughts on hold. But he was coming for a date, so I'd have to pay attention and seem not only interested but interesting.

My first impulse was to say, fuck it. Let the task force do whatever they could. But it wasn't just me they'd be taking down. They'd be taking down Connors, too. And not only had he turned out to be pretty decent to me, he was a good partner and a good friend to Harker. Getting him in trouble had all sorts of wrong written all over it. Maybe Owen would have some suggestions. I was picking up the phone to see if the answering service would page him when there was a knock at the door.

Joseph smiled at me when I answered, and I couldn't stop myself from smiling back. I was happy to see him. He wore a simple baby blue Oxford shirt, a new pair of jeans, and a windbreaker with a racing stripe down one side. He had a brown paper bag in one hand. I stepped forward, took the bag, and kissed him whether he liked it or not. He jumped a little but then he kissed me back.

"Where should we go for dinner?" I asked. As soon as I asked I felt stupid. He didn't know the neighborhood. I did. I should have picked out a place.

"There's a Mexican place on Halsted I want to try. La Mañana… I can't say it, I'll just mangle it."

"La Mañana?" It wasn't the name but I decided to go with his mispronunciation. "We had Mexican yesterday."

He shrugged. "I liked it."

"Okay, La Mañana it is."

"And we have to hurry, the movie is at nine."

"What are we seeing?" I asked.

"*Terms of Endearment*. It just won all these Oscars. And it's close."

"All right." I kind of liked that he'd made all these decisions. I certainly wasn't in the mood to be deciding things. Maybe I'd ask him to pick out my dinner for me. Maybe I'd ask him to decide what to do about Connors and the task force, too.

As we walked out of my building, I asked, "How was your counseling session?"

"Tiring."

"Well, you are struggling for your soul."

"It would be an easier struggle if I understood what winning meant. What about you? Have you struggled for your soul?"

I almost made a joke about not having a soul, but then I decided to go with a more truthful answer. "Every day."

"And how was today's struggle?"

"Bad. I'm in a tough spot. I'm working on a case for someone who's been kind to me and who's paying me a lot of money, but if I keep doing that I risk hurting myself and someone else who's been kind to me, badly, very badly."

"Can you make a different choice?" he asked.

"What do you mean?"

"You presented the situation in an either-or fashion. I'm asking if there are other options, other possibilities."

"I'm going to have to think about that."

That settled it. He was choosing my dinner.

We arrived at the restaurant. It was a narrow storefront on the corner of Halsted and Brompton. Inside, there were only about ten tables. The walls were plastered white and hung with sombreros. We ordered a couple of big slushy margaritas and munched on chips while we talked. Joseph asked how I became a private investigator, which led to my telling the story of Daniel and the bashing and how I left the CPD. I tried not to bring up Harker, though there was, eventually, something of an overlap. I decided one depressing story was enough for the evening. Somewhere along the line I made Joseph order; he chose the chicken mole for me and adventurously picked the fish special for himself. The food arrived and I had a very odd revelation.

"This is a normal date, isn't it?"

"Of course it's a normal date," Joseph said. "What other kinds are there?"

"I don't really do this."

"You don't do this? But you've had relationships. How did you get into them?"

"Well…it's kind of sex first, talk later. I mean, I dated women when I was in the closet. In fact, I dated Daniel's sister. He came over to tell me that she was seeing someone else and the two of us ended up in bed. Eventually, we did things like having dinner and seeing movies but that's not how it started."

"And with Bert?"

"I met him on a case I was working. I had a broken leg, he came over to see how I was doing and we ended up…"

"I'm sensing a theme. Both relationships started with the other guy coming over to your place and having sex."

"It's a good thing I'm homeless then…"

"Getting into another relationship would be a bad thing?" he asked.

"Relationships are challenging. Even when they're good."

"You don't strike me as the kind of guy who likes to take the easy way out of anything." He threw the statement out like it was a gauntlet.

Later, as we walked down to The Broadway Theatre just below Belmont, I turned the tables on him and managed to extract a story about his seminary days when he fell in love with one of the other students. Nothing much happened between them except for angst and longing and guilt. It would have been a better story with some real sex.

"Would you have done something if he'd been willing?" I asked.

"Yes, of course. I loved him."

"Why did you stay then? Why become a priest? If you knew that about yourself?"

"I didn't know that it was something about me. I thought it was the two of us. I didn't know it would ever happen again."

We were silent for a moment. The implication was that it was happening again, and with me. I wondered for a moment if I should do something about that—like jump out of the ticket line and run away. But I knew I wanted to fuck him. After that, I wasn't sure what I wanted to do with him. And the only way to figure that out was to hang around.

The Broadway Theatre was a second-run house built in the twenties, but it wasn't one of the gorgeous theaters like the Chicago Theatre or the Music Box. It didn't have any interesting embellishments like painted ceilings or ornate moldings. All it had were red velvet curtains and electric lights on the wall that flickered like candles. We picked seats in the back. It was a Wednesday and the movie had been out for a while so it wasn't crowded. I took my overcoat off and threw it over a seat. I wondered if I should begin wearing a gun again. I didn't want to.

Guns were for killing people and I wasn't interested in doing that again. But…I *was* being threatened. Right now they were trying to use the system to take me down. But if that didn't work, what would they do next?

Then something hit me. What exactly had I done? I'd spent weeks reading the files. Files they'd clearly wanted Jimmy's attorney's to have. The only two things I'd done outside of that was talk to The Nose Jr. and Jimmy. I could see why they didn't want me talking to anyone in the Nitti family, didn't want me to find out they'd tried to coerce testimony. But still, they were awfully quick on the trigger. I'd just been to the Nitti's that afternoon. Had they been planning something like this for the last month? Waiting until I truly started an investigation? And, if this was what they were willing to do to me, what would they do to Nitti's son in order to get what they wanted?

Joseph pressed his leg against mine. "You got quiet."

"Sorry. I was thinking about work."

"You want to talk about it some more? We could call it confession and then my vow of silence will protect your confidentiality."

I laughed. "How sweet of you to offer to pervert the rules of your religion for me."

"Confession is an opportunity to unburden. I always let people talk about whatever bothered them. It wasn't all sin all the time."

The lights went down. The previews began. I said, "I just need to think about something else for a while." And then I slipped my hand into his lap. I half expected him to move my hand away, but he didn't. I gave him a good squeeze. His dick was already swelling. It seemed like it might be impressively long, if not a bit thin. I imagined it must be very pink to match his skin. I wondered if it was freckled.

The previews were all for movies that were playing elsewhere: a new Tarzan movie, a mermaid movie, something with Jodie Foster. I explored Joseph's crotch through all of them. He moved his hand to my thigh and caressed it. His breathing grew heavy. A preview played for a new Dudley Moore movie. I didn't catch the name because I was busy pulling down Joseph's zipper. He stopped me. He had a point I suppose. This wasn't the kind of theater where guys did that. Still, I was stubborn.

I took my coat off the back of the seat in front of me and spread it across our laps. Worst-case scenario, if an usher showed up waving a flashlight at us, I could claim that we were cold. Joseph's eyes followed me as I reached under the coat and went for his zipper again. This time he let me pull it down and slip my hand into his jeans. His dick was fully hard now, as was mine. When I wrapped my hand around him, he moved his hand from my thigh to my crotch. He took hold of me through my jeans.

I was jerking him gently as the movie began. Pulling him out of his pants, I kept stroking, focusing a lot of attention on the tip. He gripped me tighter. I glanced around the theater to make sure no one had noticed what we were doing. There wasn't anyone near enough to see us in the dark.

From the corner of my eye, I could see Shirley MacLaine trying to climb into a baby's crib. I leaned over to kiss Joseph. That was even more daring than what I was doing with my hand. Anyone could turn around and see us. But still, I wanted to kiss him, wanted to kiss him while I had his dick in my hand and his hand on mine. He pulled his head back, clearly afraid, but then he leaned back in and kissed me. We explored each other with our tongues, and our hands kept up their business. I could feel his dick getting even harder and thought he might be close to coming. When the lights came up, my first horrible thought was that we'd been caught.

Immediately we separated. Joseph quickly pulled his cock back into his pants. I looked around and saw a slobby, middle-aged guy coming down the aisle. Luckily, he walked right by us. When he was halfway down the aisle he began to speak at the top of his voice, "Ladies and Gentlemen, we need to evacuate the theater as quickly as possible. Please move to the exit closest to you. There's nothing to worry about. We've just had a bomb threat called in. These are always pranks. The police will be here in a few minutes. It should take about twenty minutes for them to examine the theater and then we will restart the feature. In recognition of your patience we will be giving out free popcorn and soda when you return. Once again, please move calmly to the exits."

Half the theater was empty before he got around to offering us free popcorn. Joseph and I went out through the lobby, since that was our closest exit. Most of the audience was congregating in front of the theater, which was not a good place to stand if there actually were a bomb about to go off. But it seemed no one believed the threat. Certainly, the manager's speech gave the feeling this happened on a regular basis.

Before the CPD arrived, Joseph asked, "You don't really want to see the movie, do you?"

"I was enjoying it."

"You weren't paying any attention."

"That doesn't mean I wasn't enjoying myself. It's a comedy, right?"

"Sort of," he said. "The daughter gets cancer and dies."

"That sounds hysterical."

"See, you don't want to see it."

I shrugged. "You're right. After you've been through it a couple of times, watching people die isn't as entertaining as it used to be. We could go back to my office and continue what we were doing."

"No. I shouldn't. That was more than I'm ready for."

"You seemed ready to me." He frowned at me so I said, "All right. Whatever you want. So, we'll have another normal date, soon?"

"Yes. I'd like that."

We stared at each other. It would have been nice to kiss him again, but the street was well lit and crowded.

"So, I'll catch a cab then," he said.

"All right." It felt weird to just leave him there. "Um…so, are you okay with what we did? You don't need to talk about it?"

"I'm okay."

"I didn't push too hard did I?"

"You pushed just fine." He got a funny smile on his face and said, "I will tell you one thing. I'll never think of Shirley MacLaine the same way, that's for sure."

Then he stepped out into the street to hail a cab.

Chapter Ten

That night I slept like I was drowning in a shallow pool of water. Brian's couch was too short and too hard, and my mind was too full of bad things. Everything blended into a muddle. Jimmy English knew Madeline's secret but wouldn't tell me. Shirley MacLaine was on trial for smothering her daughter in a crib and I was supposed to help her. Someone wanted to hurt me but I couldn't see who it was. Joseph, Joseph was kissing me, touching me, feeling my cock. Was it Joseph? Or was it, I couldn't see…

I woke up. The blanket had fallen off me. My prick was hard and sticking out of my boxers. Terry sat on the coffee table just a foot away from me staring at it. I jumped up to a sitting position. Shoved my erection back into my underwear and pulled the blanket up off the floor and across my lap.

"What the fuck do you think you're doing?"

"It's more interesting than morning TV."

I wrapped the blanket around my waist and walked through the apartment until I got to Brian's door. I pounded on it, and a moment later Brian and Franklin were standing in front of me half dressed. "I woke up with a woody hanging out of my boxers and Terry was staring at it."

"But he didn't touch it?" Brian asked. "I mean, that's an improvement. Right?"

"What do you mean that's an improvement?"

Brian shrugged. "He's crawled into bed with me."

"What?" Franklin nearly jumped out of his skin.

"I told him to get out of my room," Brian said.

"You can't—this is not a safe situation," Franklin said. I wanted to disagree but I couldn't. "If anyone found out they'd blame you. And a kid like that could say anything and then where would you be?"

"Nothing's going on. He's just confused."

"I'm standing right here," Terry said from a few feet down the hall.

"Go back in the living room," I said. He didn't budge.

"It doesn't matter if nothing's going on," Franklin sputtered. "Normal people already think we rape children. Even the suggestion—"

"I'm a normal person," Brian said.

"You know what I meant."

"Yeah, you meant straight people are normal and we're not."

"That's not important now. What's important is that you're in danger and you're not seeing it."

I really hated that Franklin was right. I didn't like him and preferred that people I didn't like always be wrong.

"Terry, get dressed. Grab some of your stuff," I said.

"Oh Nick, I can't throw him out."

"You're not throwing him out. He's just going on a little vacation."

"What?" Terry practically screamed. "Where am I going?"

"You'll see."

"No. I won't do it."

"Yes you will. If you won't pack your stuff, I'll do it for you." Something about my tone of voice must have scared him because he went into his room. I went out to the living room and put on my clothes from the night before. Again the idea that I needed to get my own place crossed my mind. I really did need to do that. And not just because of Terry. Brian and Franklin were arguing in his bedroom. I already knew I didn't want to be in the middle of their relationship. As arrogant and unpleasant as I thought Franklin was, he did have Brian's interest at heart so I expected them to get through the nasty fight they were having.

Terry presented himself in the living room wearing his school uniform and carrying a backpack. "I'm not sure you'll get to school today."

"That's one good thing."

He followed me out of the apartment and down the stairs to the street. My car was a block away and Terry didn't say a thing until we got there. When we did he informed me, "You'd better not be taking me back to my parents. They'll just laugh in your face."

"Don't worry. I thought up something worse."

"Worse than my par—" I didn't hear the rest of what he said, since I'd gotten into the car. I leaned over the passenger seat and unlocked his door. He settled himself in the seat and asked, "How long do I have to be wherever the fuck you're taking me?"

"Until you learn to stop making passes at grown men."

"I didn't make a pass at you. I was just looking."

"Well it didn't make me happy to wake up and find you gawking at me like I was your own personal porno flick."

"What was I supposed to do?"

"Leave the room. Put a blanket over me. Have some common decency."

"You're an asshole."

"Then you won't mind not seeing me for a few days, will you?"

I pulled out of the parking space and went around the block so I could cut back to Lincoln and start heading northwest. I began a lecture that I hoped would last the entire drive. "Two years, Terry. You just have to wait two years and then you can fuck any guy who'll have you. You want to fuck old men in two years, have at it. But right now messing around with anyone over eighteen is just a really bad idea. And I don't mean a bad idea for you; I mean a bad idea for Brian. Brian has gone out on a limb for you and you repay him by climbing into bed with him?

Do you have any idea what happens to people who get caught with teenagers? Wait, yes, you do. You know exactly what's going to happen to Deacon DeCarlo. He's going to prison. Do you want Brian to go to prison?"

"I didn't think he'd do anything with me."

"So why did you have to try?"

"To find out."

I was quiet for half a dozen blocks, then I said, "Why can't you leave some things to find out when you turn eighteen?"

"Stop saying eighteen. The age of consent in Illinois is seventeen."

"How did you find that out?" I asked, hoping to prove him wrong. I really hoped there would be two years before this child was unleashed on the world.

"I went to the library."

I could already tell parenthood wasn't for me. The fact that the kid went to the library was terrific. The fact that he went there to find out how soon he could legally have sex was not. I couldn't think of anything else to say, so we didn't say anything the rest of the ride. When we got to Devon, I turned west and headed out to Edison Park. Ten minutes later we pulled up in front of the yellow brick condos that were now very familiar to me.

"Who lives here?" Terry asked, his voice dripping with suspicion.

"Someone I want you to meet."

"I'm not staying here if I don't want to," Terry said. "I don't have to. I'm emancipated."

"As long as you have a place to live you're emancipated. The minute you're homeless you're a ward of the state. You can stay where I put you or you can try foster care," Actually, he could only be someplace that a judge approved, but since I'd orchestrated his staying with Brian I figured he had an inflated sense of my power, so why not use it? He was silent as we walked into the lobby of Mrs. Harker's building. I buzzed her condo and a fraction of a second later she came out in an overcoat and carrying a purse. As she opened the outer door so gave me a sly look. "Is Thursday. Why you here?"

"I brought you something," I said, indicating Terry.

"Is boy." Her tone suggested she'd rather have something useful, like a head of cabbage.

"Yes. I'm hoping he can stay with you."

"Oh come on. I don't want to stay with her."

"You don't have a choice at the moment. If you behave you'll have choices."

"Wait. He not stay here. Is not place for boy."

"You did a good job with Harker. Maybe you can help me out with this one."

She eyed me suspiciously. A compliment that evoked her son. I was pulling out all the stops. She dragged me inside and let the outer door shut, leaving Terry outside.

"Where his parents?"

"They threw him out?"

"Why? Is terrible boy?"

"He's gay."

I watched a series of emotions pass over her face. Distaste. We didn't discuss gay things so I'd crossed a boundary. Sadness. Gay was like Harker. Confusion. She was probably responsible for Harker being in the closet most of his life, but she would never have thrown him out. Anger. Yup, in Eva Harker's world you do not throw boys out for any reason. "Fine. I will take."

"Thank you."

She opened the door and said, "Come, put bag in house. Then we go to church."

"Oh my God, how long do I have to stay here?" he whined, but he put his backpack into Mrs. Harker's apartment.

"I'll be here for Easter Sunday. We'll talk about it then."

"Four days, okay."

"No, not four days. Four days and we'll talk about it."

"Is time to go. Must catch bus."

"Do you want a ride?"

"No. We take bus."

"Okay."

I lit a cigarette and watched them walk down the street heading back toward Devon. Terry looked back at me a few times and I could feel him cursing me even from a block away. It was about eight o'clock in the morning and I badly needed breakfast and coffee. I also needed a shower, so I figured it was a bad idea to just grab some breakfast and start my day. I found a Dunkin Donuts on Peterson Avenue, bought a dozen mixed and three coffees, then made my way back to Brian's.

When I walked into the apartment balancing the tray of take-out coffee it seemed silent at first. Then, after a few moans drifted up my way, I realized there was make-up sex going on in the back. A couple years ago I would have walked back to Brian's bedroom and offered my assistance with the making up. The fact that I didn't like Franklin much wouldn't have stopped me for a moment. Things had changed. Things had changed a lot. I sat down at the dining room table, picked out a coffee, and chose a chocolate cake donut out of the box. I began to contemplate how I should spend my day.

The highest priority for my day was talking to Owen Lovejoy, Esquire. I needed to tell him about Connor's phone call. But since it had to do with Jimmy's case, and some very incriminating information about me, we had to meet someplace that wasn't bugged. Which meant Owen wouldn't trust the telephone, my office, or even his office. So, how exactly should I set up a meeting with him? I could call him and ask if he wants to fuck, but since someone else was in his bed last time I talked to him he'd likely say no. Not to mention, as horny as I was, I wasn't sure I was in the mood, if, in addition to the conversation about business, he expected me to follow through.

Of course, if I was going to meet with Owen I should collect my thoughts about the Levine case. He'd ask about that one too. So, where was I? There were still people I needed to talk to. The rest of the Levine family, for one. And of course, I needed to find Emily Fante.

Brian came into the dining room in his briefs. "Hey," he said when he saw me. "You're back."

"I bought donuts and coffee. Coffee's probably cold."

He looked through the box for a donut. "Where's Terry?"

"He's staying with Mrs. Harker for a few days."

"Won't she hate that?"

"If she runs true to form she'll start complaining about how awful it is in about three days, but when I try to take him back she won't want to let him go."

"*He's* going to hate it." He picked out a jelly donut and bit into it, getting purple jelly all over his chin.

"He doesn't have a lot of choices."

Franklin walked into the dining room. He wore just a towel. He wasn't bad looking. Maybe I'd made a mistake foregoing a three-way I wasn't invited to. He saw me and blushed. "What's going on?"

"Nick brought Terry out to Mrs. Harker's"

"Who's Mrs. Harker?"

Brian opened his mouth to give a full explanation but then thought better of it. "A friend," he finally said. "He's not going to stay there long, right Nick?"

"You can't let him come back here," Franklin said.

"Well, he's not going to like it with Mrs. Harker," Brian explained. "She's in her seventies or something. And sort of a bitch."

"That doesn't make any difference. It's not safe if you're here. I'm surprised a judge let it happen in the first place."

"Because all gay men want is to have sex with children?" I asked.

"Because that's what straight people think."

"And the best way to get them to not think that is to avoid all contact with children?"

"Yes, absolutely," Franklin said emphatically. He suddenly made me feel like all gay teachers were incredibly brave people.

"I'm not going to abandon Terry," Brian said. "He needs to learn to behave himself, that's all. Let's see what a few days with Mrs. Harker does for him."

"It might take more than that," I pointed out. "Franklin, have a donut."

"Oh, I couldn't. All that fat."

"There's cold coffee, too," I added.

"Thank you, Nick," Brian said. "I'm the one who took responsibility for him, you really didn't have to do anything."

"I brought him here. That means I did."

Franklin looked from me to Brian and back again. He didn't look happy. I got the impression that it wasn't exactly me he didn't like; it seemed as though he didn't like that Brian and I were friends. I also got the impression that Brian might not have completely explained how things were between us. He could have said that I was a friend of his ex who needed a place to stay. That was completely true, but left out so much it was also a lie.

"Well, I need to take a shower if the bathroom is free."

I gathered my things and went into the bathroom. I gave myself the whole shower to worry about where I should live. I had much bigger problems at the moment so I couldn't afford to be thinking about it all day. I needed to move. Not just because of Franklin. But because Brian deserved to be able to bring a guy home without having their first conversation be about me. "Yes, I fuck Nick occasionally and I care about him but we both know things are going nowhere," is a turnoff for a lot of guys. Of course, since there was also someone who wanted to pin a murder on me, and especially since it was a murder I actually committed, finding a new place to live needed to be easy and hassle free.

It was hard to imagine a life where anything was hassle free.

Chapter Eleven

Speaking of hassles, when I arrived at my office a half an hour later, Christian Baylor stood in my doorway. He wore a parka and held an umbrella in one hand. The streets looked as though it had rained overnight, and above us the dark, heavy clouds threatened to let loose again.

"I'm not happy to see you," I said when I reached him. It was an understatement.

"A policeman came to see me," he said, following me into the stairwell.

"Yeah, what was his name?"

"Devlin. Harry Devlin. I think he said he was a captain."

"What did he want?"

"To talk to me about the story I wrote."

I unlocked my office door and walked in. "Yeah, congratulations on that. I read it. I guess I should have sent you a note or something. It was a stunning piece of journalistic fiction."

"I didn't think you'd want me writing about you so I left you out. Big deal."

"You're right. I didn't want you writing about me. I didn't want you writing about Bert either."

"I have a right to my own experiences."

"Half of which you made up."

He shook his head dismissively. "It doesn't matter, Nick. It's in the past. This Captain Devlin...he was scary."

"But that's why it does matter. If you hadn't written the article you wouldn't be getting visits from scary policemen."

"He wanted to know who the vigilante was who killed Gorshuk. I didn't tell him anything."

"You don't know anything. I hope you told him that."

"But I do know something."

"Yeah, what do you know?"

"I talked to an officer who was there on the scene when they found Gorshuk's body. They found a gun in the cemetery. They sent the serial number out to be identified, and then a day later the gun disappeared and it was like the report was never requested. The guy who picked it up and turned it in only remembers that it was a Sig Sauer."

"So what?"

"I know you have a Sig Sauer."

"Do you?"

"I asked Bert about what kinds of guns cops like. He told me about his Smith and Wesson. Then he mentioned you carried a Sig Sauer."

"You're absolutely right. I have the only Sig Sauer in Chicago."

"I know a lot of people have those guns. But how many of those people would have been in Graceland cemetery the night the Bughouse Slasher died?"

"Is that it?" I asked.

"What?"

"Is that all the information you have?"

"Yes."

"Then you should go."

He got a pouty look on his face. "You always hated me. I've never understood why."

"Really? Re-read your article. That might tell you why."

He tossed his head with a little huff and walked out of my office.

I checked my messages. There were three hang-ups. Sooner or later I was going to have to plunk myself down in my office for at least four or five hours so I could pick up the phone when that person called back. It wasn't, however, going to be that morning. What I needed to do that morning was talk to Owen Lovejoy, Esquire. I just had to figure out how.

I had no idea how many resources the Feds were devoting to this. I knew there was equipment you could get that you could aim at people in parks and places and pick up at least part of their conversation. Coppola made a movie in the early seventies where they did exactly that. Though, being in the business, it's hard to imagine a client paying the kind of invoices something like that would generate. Which is part of why I doubted the Feds were doing anything of the sort. The CIA might have that kind of gear to keep an eye on the Russians, but I really didn't think the FBI could get that kind of expense approved to take down an elderly mobster. Particularly when they didn't even have a warrant.

I decided to head downtown. The paper bag full of Joseph's black suit and collar sat on my sofa. I thought about taking it with me and beginning my surveillance after I met with Owen, but I hadn't shaved. I looked too unkempt to be a priest. I needed to pull myself together, maybe even get a haircut before I began. Interesting that impersonating someone who might have taken a vow of poverty required that I not look shabby.

A half an hour later, I was getting off an elevator and walking into the penthouse offices of Cooke, Babcock and Lackerby. The offices were in a turn-of-the-century nineteen-story building on Jackson. Ironically, the building was two blocks from the Federal building where Operation Tea and Crumpets was housed.

The lobby was traditional "lawyer": paneled, British prints of horses and hounds, a heavy walnut reception desk. The receptionist was pretty, brunette, and wore a very conservative blouse and skirt. She plucked away at an IBM Selectric doing double duty as a typist. She looked up at me and was about to say something when I put my finger to my mouth. I reached over her desk and grabbed a pad that was sitting there and a pen. She looked at me curiously, a little offended.

On one sheet, I wrote: GIVE THIS TO MR. LOVEJOY. On a second, I wrote: WE NEED TO MEET. I'M IN THE RECEPTION AREA. NICK. When she read the second note she frowned at me. "He might be busy, you know. They usually are." I wagged a finger in the general direction of his office. She rolled her eyes and walked through the arch that led to the offices.

Standing alone in the reception area, I worried that the task force might have put cameras in the room somewhere but that seemed unlikely. Yeah, the Feds used cameras in some of their cases, like the DeLorean case and the ABSCAM thing, but they always had to have control of the environment. Those stings took place in hotel rooms with technicians in the next room. They wouldn't have been able to get cameras into a law firm's reception area.

God, I thought, *I'm getting paranoid.*

I also wondered if I needed to find out more about this stuff. The Feds had put a bug into a lawyer's office and probably tapped their phones. In response, I was planning to dress like a priest and stand in a lobby. I felt like I was behind the eight ball. I knew it wasn't legal for me to put a bug in the task force offices. In Illinois you couldn't even record a phone call without both party's consent. But still, I should at least learn how to check a room for bugs.

The receptionist returned with a surprised look on her face. She didn't say anything to me, just sat back down at her desk. Then Owen Lovejoy, Esquire came into the lobby wearing a trench coat over his expensive suit. Silently, we walked out of the office and back to the elevator. On the way down, we didn't say anything, though I imagine it would have been safe. When we got out to Jackson, we walked toward the lake.

"So you're sure your office is bugged?"

"Yeah, we had a guy come out and check. It's on the underside of one of my guest chairs. There are also bugs in the offices of Mr. Cooke, Mr. Babcock, Mr. Lackerby, the reception area and the men's room. They're very thorough."

"Why not remove the bugs?"

"We don't want them to know we know, for one thing. For another they'll just put them back and try harder next time."

"Are you sure we can't get them on that? You want me to look into it?"

"What you're doing is too important. And it means I control what they know. Jimmy comes down once a week, sits in Mr. Babcock's office, and they tell each other dirty jokes for an hour."

"And that doesn't tell them you know there's a bug?"

"Mr. Babcock charges three hundred and fifty dollars an hour. Clients get to talk about whatever they want."

"I can't believe they pull shit like this," I said. Part of me wanted the good guys to be good and the bad guys to be bad. It just made life easier.

Owen shrugged. "Twenty years ago Johnson told the FBI to stop with the illegal wiretaps. But presidents change. Time passes and they're back to their old tricks." An idea hit him. "Do you know if Jimmy has bugged the task force? Is this why you wanted to see me? Wiretapping?"

"No. As far as I know Jimmy hasn't done anything like that. And you don't want to know if he has."

Technically, lawyers weren't supposed to break the law any more than Federal agencies.

I decided to tackle the uncomfortable bit of what I needed to tell him first. "I went to see Jimmy."

"I would have liked to have known that before you did it."

"I was out in the suburbs anyway and I couldn't exactly call you and tell you, now could I?" I hadn't thought of it at the time, but it made a good excuse now.

"Still, I'd like to know these things, dear."

"I know."

"What did you talk to him about?" Owen asked, as we crossed Michigan Avenue. I scanned the people nearby, attempting to be sure we weren't being followed. Feeling really paranoid while I did it.

"I wanted to make sure he didn't keep any kind of a diary. And I wanted him to be thinking about people who might have."

"That was on my list for our next conversation. I'll follow-up."

"I went to see Nino Nitti's son, Nino Jr. I was trying to see his widow but she's senile and doesn't remember who she is half the time. The son said the Feds were there putting pressure on him to say that his father confessed that Jimmy hired him to kill the Perellis."

"Is he going to say that?"

"I don't think so. He seemed pissed about it."

"Do you think I can get him to talk about their trying to put words in his mouth?"

"You can try. But that will probably piss him off, too. He just wants to go back to Indianapolis."

"What are you doing next?"

"There's more I need to tell you." We stopped walking and stood in front of the Art Institute by the southerly lion. I don't know why I knew this, but I seemed to remember that the lion was named Defiance. "It's not good. I got a call from Detective Frank Connors. He was Harker's partner."

"Okay," Owen said, not really seeing a connection.

"He also handled the Bughouse Slasher investigation. This morning I had a visit from Christian Baylor. He wrote an article about the Slasher. There's a CPD Captain named Devlin looking into the death of the Slasher."

"Devlin is on the task force," Owen said, getting half the connection.

"You're still my attorney, right?"

"Of course."

"The night Joseph Gorshuk was killed my gun was found in the cemetery. Connors returned it to me."

Owen's mind raced with the various possibilities. "Oh. I see. So this Devlin guy is coming after you because you're working for Jimmy now."

"Exactly. And he'll take down Connors in the process."

"Nick, the safest thing to do is to walk away. They'll leave you alone if you back off. Jimmy will understand and so will I."

I thought about it for a moment. I remembered Joseph saying that I should try to make a different choice if

I could. I wanted to make a different choice, I just didn't know what—something occurred to me. I looked at Owen and said, "Let's go back to your office."

"And do what?"

"Control what the task force knows."

On the walk back, I explained exactly what I wanted to do. Which was basically to repeat much of what I'd said, then quit, or rather pretend to quit and keep right on working for Jimmy. It would take them a while to figure out I was still working but it might give me enough time to find something out.

We walked into the reception area of Cooke, Babcock and Lackerby, and the receptionist looked up at us in surprise. She couldn't figure out why we'd gone to such lengths to not speak in Owen's office and were now going to do exactly that. I gave her a sympathetic smile as we walked by.

In Owen's office, I sat down on one of the thin, metal chairs and pointed back and forth, silently asking which one was bugged. Owen pointed at the one I wasn't sitting in. I leaned in that direction. Owen sat down and said, "Nick! How are you doing?" I nearly cringed. He wasn't much of an actor.

"Not so great." Actually, I wasn't much of an actor either. "I've heard from a couple of people that a cop is chasing down my tail. A guy named Devlin."

"There's a guy named Devlin on Operation Tea and Crumpets."

"Same guy. He's got me on something I did. Something incriminating."

"What exactly?"

"I'd rather not say. Even to my attorney."

"So…are you quitting?"

That threw me a little. It was sort of my line. "Um, yeah. I have to."

"But you can still work on the Levine case, right?"

"Yes, absolutely."

"Jimmy's going to be very angry." That was good. It fit into their idea of Jimmy as an angry, mean person.

"I know, but I don't want to end up in prison."

"I'll do my best to make Jimmy understand."

"I appreciate that."

Owen raised an index finger. Then wrote a note. It said, "BUY A BEEPER." While I read that he said, "Keep me up-to-date on the Levine case."

"I will." Though I hadn't updated him and perhaps should have done just that.

He handed me another note on which there was a phone number. I mouthed the word, BEEPER? And he nodded. Then I said goodbye and walked out of his office. All in all, I thought we'd just done a very good job of misdirection. I decided I'd spend the rest of the day on the Levine case, just in case I was being followed around. Taking the day off from Jimmy's case lent truth to the lie.

Before I left the Loop I looked around for a place to get a beeper. It seemed like these places were springing up all over the place, but then when I wanted one I had trouble finding it. I finally found one on Madison a few doors down from the French Bakery where Brian still worked. It was getting close to eleven so he'd be just getting there. I wondered if Franklin came with him.

These past few days Franklin seemed to be everywhere Brian was.

I spent forty-five grueling minutes in the store. By the time I was done I felt mugged. Worse, my mugger was going to mug me to the tune of twenty-five dollars a month for as long as I carried the little black plastic box around. On the upside, when the salesman spent five minutes trying to sell me a briefcase telephone that cost nearly four thousand dollars I managed not to punch him. I had a lot of trouble understanding why I desperately needed something that hadn't even existed a few years ago. I thought I'd been getting by just fine without a beeper. Now, people would be able to reach me any time, anywhere. I wasn't sure I liked that idea.

Chapter Twelve

After deciding not to have lunch at the French Bakery, I caught the El back to Boystown. My plan was to grab my car and head out to Park Ridge. I figured I'd find a diner somewhere and have some lunch. On the way from the Belmont El station to Roscoe where my car was parked, I stopped at my office. I called the receptionist at Cooke, Babcock and Lackerby, told her my pager number and asked her to give it to Owen.

I remembered a diner out in Lincoln Square that was mediocre at best but had parking nearby and the guarantee of an open table. The place was called Tasty Bites; it had an overwhelming and encyclopedic menu, so I started thinking about what I might want for lunch well before I got there. After the loose-boned waitress sat me in a booth next to the window, she began to walk away. I said, "I know what I want."

"Really? Usually it takes people forever." She took out a pad.

"I'd like a grilled ham and cheese, with French fries and a Coca-Cola."

"What kind of bread?"

"White."

"What kind of cheese?"

"Cheddar."

"You want a salad with that?"

I raised an eyebrow.

"They make me ask."

"No I don't want a salad, but why don't we count talking about it toward my daily requirements."

"Funny," she said, without enthusiasm. She snatched up the menu and loped off.

I lit a cigarette and tried to get my focus back on the Levine case. Most of my adult life I'd done more than one thing at a time. When I was on the job I only worked for the CPD, but my life at home with Daniel was like a completely different world. It was like being two people. Then when I left the CPD, I started working as an investigator, but for a long time it wasn't enough money so I was a doorman two nights a week at Paradise Isle, a disco that had eventually shut down. I think someone was turning the place into a mattress store. Anyway, I felt like I should be a lot better at juggling everything I had going on. Yeah, there was a lot at stake in Jimmy's case and not just for Jimmy. And there was a lot at stake with Madeline's case, though it wasn't as personal to me. Probably since I'd never met her and to me she was little more than a picture in the newspaper.

My sandwich arrived and it was pretty good. Though it seemed hard to screw up. The greasier and soggier the better. The same cannot be said for the French fries. They were also greasy and soggy, but that doesn't work for fries. I ate them anyway, paid my bill, and got back on the road.

The Levine's lived in a grand two-story brick house with brilliant white trim and delicate lace curtains. The lawn was winter brown and the trees were naked. As nice as the house was, it looked beaten down, as though it were reacting to the stress of Madeline's trial. As I got to the front door it opened and a black woman came out dressed in a sweatshirt and a pair of jeans. Closing the door behind her, she carried a bucket filled with cleaning supplies. She walked past me without smiling. I rang the bell.

The door opened quickly. A woman in her early sixties with a gray pageboy looked at me with a bit of surprise then glowered over my shoulder at her maid.

"Why do I always feel guilty when she comes? I pay her twelve dollars an hour and she doesn't even do that good a job. I'm helping her feed her family, but every time she comes I feel like I'm doing her some terrible disservice. Who are you?"

"My name is Nick Nowak." I handed her a card. "I'm working with your daughter's attorneys on her case."

"That's over, isn't it?"

"We're working on the sentencing phase."

"I've already told Maddy's lawyers I can't testify."

"I know. I'd just like to talk to you about avenues we could pursue to help lessen your daughter's sentence."

Her nose crinkled. At first, I thought it was in distaste at the idea of helping her daughter, then she asked, "Do you smoke?"

That was embarrassing, she'd just smelled me. "Yes, I'm sorry if—"

"I'll let you in for ten minutes if you give me a cigarette."

"Deal."

She led me into the house. We walked past a living room where two small children sat in front of a television watching a *Tom and Jerry* cartoon. They were younger than I'd remembered, a boy and a girl around three and five. Mrs. Levine glanced at the TV and said, "There's about twenty minutes left on that tape so we should be fine. They won't move until it's over." Then she led me down the hallway to the kitchen, which was enormous and spotlessly clean. Looked to me like the maid did a damn fine job.

"My daughter hates the idea of me smoking around her children. I smoked around her when she was a child and it didn't do anything to her. Well, I guess that's debatable."

I pulled out my pack of Marlboro's and flipped the lid back to offer her one. We each lit up and stood in front of the sink using it as an ashtray.

"So you're here to get me to testify for my daughter."

"That's not what I said."

"I know what you said. The thing is, I don't know what I'd say. I can't go into court and say that Wes deserved to die. He didn't. I can't say my daughter needs to be with her children because she's a good mother. She's not. I've been raising her children for her all along. The only difference is now it's official. Now I have a legal right. I can't think of one honest thing I could say that would help her."

"You could say you love her."

Her face froze. "Is that all it takes to keep someone out of prison? For a mother to stand up and say they're loved? Thank God you've figured that out. Now we can empty the prisons."

I thought it best to ignore that. "You testified against your daughter."

"I didn't volunteer to do that. They made me. Then they called me hostile. I wasn't hostile, I was very polite. If anyone was hostile it was the attorneys."

"Tell me about Wes. What did you think of him?"

"I thought he was great. Any mother would. He was charming and good-looking, and he made my daughter happy. And yes, he wasn't what you'd call ambitious, but Maddy had enough ambition for both of them. An ambitious man would have gotten in her way."

"So what happened?"

She shrugged and took a drag off her cigarette.

"I know about the drugs," I said. "Maddy was stealing drugs from her practice."

"Well, now you know why I can't testify."

"Was Wes using too?"

"We tried to help them both. We really did. My husband threatened to take the children away if they didn't stop. Maddy did. She began going to those meetings. She got better."

"But Wes didn't."

"No."

"Do you know who Emily Fante is?"

"No."

"She was a friend of Madeline's."

"I know all of my daughter's friends."

"Do you know her drug friends?"

"Drug friends? I don't know what that is."

"When people do drugs they make friends with people who do drugs. It makes it easier to get what you need."

"No. I don't know any of her *drug* friends."

Something occurred to me, something that struck me as odd. "How much of this was in your testimony?"

"Not much. I answered the questions I was asked. I didn't elaborate."

"What did you say?"

"They asked me about Maddy's relationship with Wes. I said it wasn't good. They made me describe several arguments they had while visiting. They asked me what the problems were in their marriage. I said I didn't know."

"The problem was drugs."

"No. The symptom was drugs. I have no idea why either of them used drugs."

"Was he having an affair?"

"I'm sure he was. Charming men usually are."

"Was he always having affairs?"

"I don't know. Maddy wouldn't tell me something like that. She liked things to at least look perfect."

She turned on the faucet and ran her cigarette butt under the stream, then dropped it into the garbage disposal. I followed suit.

"Do you think the story Maddy told was true? That Wes confessed to having an affair and she stabbed him in a rage?"

"I hope not."

"What do you mean you hope not?"

"I mean I hope all of this has a point. If Wes was having an affair, Maddy could easily have divorced him. She could even have kept him away from the kids if she wanted. At least until he stopped using drugs. And if he didn't stop. Well, he wasn't going to last long. She could have just waited."

"What do you mean?"

"He didn't look good. He'd lost a lot of weight. I mean, they don't eat right, do they? Users? And his skin wasn't good. He was getting these awful red blotches. It was sad. He'd been so handsome. He'd have been dead by now. If Maddy hadn't killed him."

After that she was finished. I offered her another cigarette but she turned it down.

There was nothing to do but drive back to my office. When I got there, I set the bag with the priest suit in it by the door so I'd remember to take it with me and I could leave from Brian's apartment in the morning. I called Owen's pager number and listened to the prompt, then I put in my office phone number for him to call me back. Then I called Joseph.

"It's nice to hear from you," he said.

"It's nice to be heard. Do you have plans for tomorrow night?"

"Let me check my dance card." He took a slight pause to support his joke. "No, it looks like I'm free."

Then I gave him my beeper number in case he needed to reach me and I wasn't in my office. As soon as I said beeper he said, "Well...everything's up to date in Kansas City."

"I beg your pardon?"

"It's from a musical. *Oklahoma.*"

"And you're just now figuring out you're gay?"

"No, I've known forever. I just thought I could choose something else. Something more important. And I still might choose that."

I didn't know what to say to that and didn't have to come with a response because call waiting beeped in. "I have to take this."

"You know who's calling?"

"I'm expecting a call. Tomorrow around six-thirty? Meet at my office? We'll figure out what to do then."

"Okay. Bye."

I switched over. Like I expected, it was Owen Lovejoy, Esquire.

"You rang?"

"I did. I saw Mrs. Levine about an hour ago."

"What was that like?"

"She's knows a lot. A lot that she managed to keep out of testimony."

"Well don't keep me in suspense, tell me."

"Madeline and Wes both had trouble with drugs. Madeline got through it for her kids. Wes didn't."

"Why didn't Madeline tell us? We could have made Wes look like a cheating drug addict, and it would have been true."

"You would have had to make her look like a drug addict too, though. The other thing is—"

"There's more? Shit."

"Mrs. Levine says that Wes was sick. She doesn't think he was long for this world anyway. Is there anything on the autopsy?"

"I'll have to dig it out. When I read it before I focused on the skill with which she killed him. She put the knife directly into his heart."

"Anatomy class."

"Exactly. Try to make a direct hit seem like it's not premeditated."

"I'm looking for signs of long-term drug abuse, liver damage, malnutrition."

"What do you think that will get us?"

"I don't know. I would like to know if Mrs. Levine is telling the truth."

"All right. I'll have a copy made for you. It'll be at the front desk."

"Thanks."

We chatted for a few minutes about the remaining names on the list he gave me. Given the direction things had gone, he told me I didn't have to bother with Madeline's father and brother unless there was something specific I was looking for. It would still be helpful to find the mistress but even that was risky. If we found her and managed to get her in the newspaper she could say some pretty damning things about Madeline and Wes' drug use. When tainting a jury pool you needed to taint it in the right direction.

"I may need to re-strategize," Owen said.

I didn't envy him.

Even though it was a little before three, I decided to call it a day. My plan was to spend Friday staking out the Federal Building's lobby. Then Saturday, I'd start looking into Wes Berkson. I had to find family, friends, co-workers. I knew he didn't have a job when he was killed, but had he worked at all in the last year of his life? I needed to find that out. I had my work cut out for me, but I figured I'd manage to talk to at least a few people on Sunday. Well, Sunday afternoon. Late Sunday afternoon. I was planning a hangover after a night at the Glorgy Hole followed by Easter dinner with Mrs. Harker and Terry.

I grabbed the bag with Joseph's suit in it and walked home. I felt uncomfortable about our "normal" date. I hadn't given a lot of thought to what we were doing. In my world, the options were sleep with him a few times and move on or, if I liked him enough, not move on. I hadn't really considered the possibility of seeing him for a while, fooling around, getting to like him, and then getting dumped for God. The whole thing was giving me a lump in my stomach. I'd had a lot of shitty things happen in the last few years and I was just starting to feel good. I didn't want anything or anyone fucking with that.

Brian worked mainly lunches at The French Bakery, which meant he was down in the Loop by ten-thirty and gone by two. Twice a week he worked dinner, usually Thursday and Friday but sometimes he traded shifts or gave them away outright. He didn't need the money he made there. In fact, I wasn't sure why he bothered to work there at all. When I was walking into the apartment I was really hoping to take a nap. But Brian was home. He and Franklin were stuffing envelopes on the dining room table and drinking white wine. A bottle of Chardonnay sat half empty on the table.

"Hey," I said.

"How are you, Nick?" Brian asked.

Franklin sat there like I hadn't entered the room.

"I'm okay. Has Terry called and asked to come home yet?"

"Twice. When can we let him come home?"

"I'm thinking Sunday. That should be long enough to make the point."

There was a sour look on Franklin's face but he kept his mouth shut. Brian seemed to relax, whether it was because he knew when Terry would be back or because he was relieved that Franklin hadn't made a comment about Terry, I couldn't be sure.

"What are you guys doing?" I asked.

"Fundraising letter for Howard Brown. Sugar bought us the mailing list from the Opera so we're doing an extra push. Opera queens." Brian rolled his eyes flamboyantly.

"Don't do that," Franklin said. "Using terms like that. It's degrading."

"What?" Brian was honestly confused.

"Don't call men queens. It's degrading to feminize men."

"Oh, Mary," I said. Not a term I normally use but he was pissing me off.

"I have a legitimate point," Franklin said, setting his jaw.

"Do you hate women?" I asked.

"Of course not."

"Then why is it degrading to feminize a man if there's nothing wrong with women?"

"You're twisting my words."

"Please don't fight," Brian said.

"I'm going to take a nap in Terry's room."

"Is that a good idea? You know how protective he is of his space."

Even though the kid wasn't there, it didn't feel right.

"Why don't you use my bed," Brian said.

"But—" Franklin started but stopped. He was protective of his space, too.

"You know, maybe I'll go for a walk. That'll wake me up."

"Oh, okay," Brian said. "Before you go, though, I'm not sure about Saturday night. Could you go with Sugar to the Glory Hole?"

"You're not sure? Why aren't you sure?"

"I don't know that Franklin's going to be very comfortable at the Glory Hole."

"I'm sorry. I'm really not used to spending a lot of time with gay people," Franklin explained. "Most of my friends are straight. I don't believe in segregating ourselves."

There were a lot of things wrong with what he said. Most importantly, did he really expect me to go down to Rush Street and try to pick up guys? I mean, the whole point of gay bars was segregation. He was viewing the segregation as a rejection by straight people, but, hey, maybe we just wanted to be alone.

"How long have the two of you been together?" I asked.

"We met two weeks ago."

The look on my face must have been very articulate because Franklin said, "I know what you're thinking. We're moving too fast. It hasn't been long, but I really care about Brian."

Brian smiled, obviously pleased.

I wanted out of the conversation so I said, "Sure. I'll take Sugar if you don't want to go. Why not?" Then I said, "See you later" and walked out of the apartment.

Chapter Thirteen

I walked toward the lake thinking I'd take a walk in the park or maybe along the Belmont Rocks. When I got to Lake Shore Drive though, I had another idea. I walked south to Two Towers, Lana Shepherd's building. In the lobby, I followed the sign to the rental office, which was set up a little like a doctor's office, with a door and a receptionist's window. Next to the window, which was frosted glass and closed, was a plastic doorbell. I rang it.

A moment later, a young woman of about twenty-five opened the window. She was odd. I noticed that right away. For one thing, she was at least six feet tall. She practically looked at me eye to eye. For another, her hair was cut in the same kind of extreme pixie cut that Mia Farrow wore in *Rosemary's Baby* and dyed flat black. This was completely out of step with what I'd seen other girls her age doing, which was to make their hair seem as big and as curly as possible. Half of them looked like they'd killed some poor woodlands creature and stuck it on their heads. So maybe this girl had the right idea.

"Can I help you?"

"How much do one-bedrooms go for?"

"Three-seventy-five to four-forty, depending on the floor." It was much more than my garden apartment had cost, but was still far less than I was making in a week. In fact, this rent and my office rent were still less than a week's wages. I was flush, too. I had most of what Jimmy had paid me for the last two months in the bank. I tried to give Brian money but he wouldn't take it. Whenever I tried to leave money on his dresser he always snuck it back into my jeans.

"Do you have anything with a view of the lake?"

"We have a tenth floor unit in the front. Hang on a second."

Behind the wall were a couple of desks sitting in a small, windowless room. She walked over to the nearest desk and looked at a sheet. She wore a sort of T-shirt that was red with cap sleeves, well-tailored blue jeans, and pair of penny loafers. I noticed she never stood up completely straight, as if trying to compensate for her height, not by slouching as many tall girls do but by leaning. She leaned to the left, to the right, and back. I don't think she was conscious of it.

"That unit is four hundred and twenty. Would you like to see it?"

"Yes. I would."

Taking the sheet with her, she walked over to a pegboard that held at least a hundred sets of keys. She pulled four sets, then walked back and closed the window. Coming through the door she said, "My name is Clementine. I'm the manager for the building. I handle showing the apartments and applications. I also direct all the maintenance. If you become a tenant you bring any problems to me." That would be strange, bringing my problems to such a young girl. But I suppose I could get used to it.

"And you are?" she asked, leading me back to the lobby.

"Nick. Nick Nowak."

"What you do for a living Mr. Nowak?"

"I'm a private investigator. You can call me Nick." Because calling me mister made me feel really old.

As we walked across the lobby to the 3220 side, we continued to chat.

"Private investigator. Is that a stable field?"

"It can be. It's very stable at the moment. I'm loosely attached to a law firm downtown, Cooke, Babcock and Lackerby."

She smiled at that. Everyone knew that anything connected to lawyers, loosely or otherwise, meant a goldmine. "How did you find us?"

"I interviewed someone in the building."

"I see. Where are you living now?"

"With a friend around the corner." That didn't sound good. "I was over on Roscoe for about four years. I left on good terms. I'm sure the landlord will give me a good recommendation."

"Are you on the lease where you are right now?"

"No. I'm on the couch."

"I see."

We walked into the elevator area of 3220. She pressed the call button. I decided I'd better say something close to the truth if I wanted her on my side. "I had some bad things happen to me last year. None of them were financial though. All my bills got paid." Mainly because I moved out of the Roscoe apartment rather abruptly, but that was fine because I hadn't been on a lease for a couple of years. The elevator arrived and she was polite enough not to pry any further. It was a nice elevator with imitation wood paneling on the walls.

"There's a service elevator around the corner for moving in and deliveries. In the basement there's a laundry room, a dry cleaner and small store where you can get, you know, this and that."

When we reached the tenth floor, we were in a hallway just like Lana Shepherd's on the fourth floor. The walls were painted a buttery yellow and there was a low pile brown carpet. We didn't wander around as I did when I tried to find Lana's apartment, Clementine knew exactly where we were going. We walked to the end of the hallway where there were three doors leading to three apartments: 1008, 1009 and 1010. She opened the door to 1008.

Empty apartments are curious places. They're full of the ghosts of past tenants and the hopes of prospective ones. The living room space was large and carpeted in chocolate brown wall-to-wall, and the walls were painted…in all honesty, they were painted the color of a cum stain. It had the same kind of kitchen in a closet arrangement as Lana's apartment. The only thing that was at all remarkable was the window. It went from the kitchen all the way across to the far wall of the living room. Probably a good twelve or thirteen feet. It began at hip height and went nearly to the ceiling. There was a white marble sill about eight inches deep.

The view was terrific. It was probably a little after six. The sun was edging off to the western horizon but it was still fairly bright out. The apartment faced north, and the building jutted out a bit from the one directly next to it, so there was a wide view of Lake Shore Drive, Lincoln Park and Lake Michigan. It was a great view.

Oddly though, looking north like that at the arching row of apartment buildings the image reminded me of the beginning of *The Jackie Gleason Show*, which showed a similar shot of Miami Beach while the announcer said, "From the sun and fun capitol of the world, Miami Beach…"

I wanted the place. I wanted it bad.

"I'll take it," I said.

"Why don't we look at the bedroom first?"

I followed her into the bedroom, which was nearly as large as the living room. It had two closets and a place for a dresser inset between them. The window was large, but not as wide as the one in the living room. The floor was tiled in marbleized brown linoleum. It was fine. It would do.

"The bathroom is right here," Clementine said and led me out of the bedroom. The bathroom sat in between the living room and the bedroom. It was small with tiny white tiles that were occasionally broken up by a colored tile, red or yellow or blue. Above the tub was a small window with a deep shelf.

"Can I say I'll take it yet?"

"Wouldn't you like to see other units? We have several floor plans."

"Do they have better views?"

"No, not really."

"Then I'll take this one."

"All right. You'll need to fill out an application. We'll need a check for first and last month's rent, so that would be eight hundred and twenty dollars."

"Can I paint if I want to?"

"We don't encourage it. But people do."

"Can I move in tomorrow?"

"Tomorrow? We usually do the first."

"I'll pay for half a month. In fact, how about I give you the deposit and the first three months. Sixteen-forty plus two-oh-five is eighteen-forty-five." Money is amazing; it smoothes over so many things.

"Um, sure, you can do that if you want."

"I want."

"Okay. Let's go fill out the application and I'll call you tomorrow."

"Morning."

She laughed. "I'll call you tomorrow morning."

When we finished it was still early so I went down to the Melrose and had a hamburger with some fries. Then I walked over to my office. On the way, I thought about the situation with Brian. Franklin wasn't *that* bad. If he liked Brian, that was terrific as long as Brian liked him. The fact that I already knew I didn't want to spend a whole lot of time with him was my problem and I'd just resolved it. Everybody was going to be a lot happier as of tomorrow. Provided the powers that be at Two Towers liked my application. Or at least my check for nearly two grand.

When I walked into my office, I immediately sat down and began a list of all the things I needed to do. I had to call and make arrangements for a phone to be put in. I didn't relish the idea of my beeper going off and having to wander over to Broadway to find a payphone. I also had to buy a bed. The one place I knew I wasn't going to buy a bed was the mattress store that now occupied Paradise Island. It felt like it would be an insult to my past to do that. It was bad enough the bar wasn't there anymore.

I'd asked if I could paint. Did I really want to do that? It was a lot of work. I'd painted the Roscoe apartment with Daniel. This one I'd be doing alone. And, if I did paint, what color did I want? Cum stain was not my favorite color. Well, in certain situations it was; just not on the walls of my apartment. Daniel had decided on gray for the old apartment. Could I ask Joseph to help me? Was he even good—

My phone rang. I picked it up and heard nothing for a moment.

"Hello? Is someone there?"

"You're looking for me?" a woman's voice slurred.

"I may be. Who is this?"

"Emily Fante."

"Yes, I have been looking for you."

"Well, come and find me."

"Come and find you where?"

"I'm at a bar on Broadway."

"Which bar on Broadway?"

"It's called The Closet."

"I know it."

"You do? That's interesting."

"Not really. I'll be there in a few minutes."

I hung up, grabbed my coat, and walked out of my office. It was a five-minute walk to The Closet. I remembered Kimmy saying that Emily looked kind of "dyke-y." Apparently, Emily might be a lesbian. The Closet was mixed, catering to both gay men and gay women. It had a neighborhood feel, and if you lived in the neighborhood you were more than welcome. Especially if you were as serious about drinking as Emily seemed to be.

Ten minutes later I walked into the storefront bar. The place was small, with half the space taken up by a horseshoe bar. As it was still early, there were only about half a dozen people in the bar. I assumed it would fill up later. Thursday was the night that people went out. If you lived in the city you avoided most bars on Friday and Saturday since they were full of suburbanites.

Sitting on the far side of the bar was a square looking woman with short hair. She was just a few years older than I was, but that fit with Kimmy's idea of "older." I walked over and asked if she was Emily Fante.

"Are you the guy who's looking for me?"

"I am. Nick Nowak. I'm an investigator working with Madeline Levine-Berkson's attorneys." I gave her my card and she set it down next to her drink.

"Can I buy you a drink?" I asked.

"Of course you can."

I asked the bartender for a Johnnie Walker Red on the rocks and whatever the lady was having. That made

Emily smirk. Well, what did she expect me to say? "And one for the bull dyke?"

"This isn't as bad as it looks," she said.

"It's not?"

"No. Not at all. This is just booze."

"Your problem is drugs?" It looked like she had bigger problems than just drugs, but I wasn't going to tell her that. "Is that how you know Madeline? From doing drugs together?"

She shook her head. "No. I'm her sponsor in NA. Narcotics Anonymous." Then she said again, "This is just booze by the way."

"I believe you."

"That's why I can't testify. All that will come out."

"That Madeline was a drug addict?"

"Yes, that she was an addict. Is an addict."

"Did you know Wes Berkson?"

She shook her head again. "Never met him. Wouldn't want to either."

"He never came to NA?"

"Never."

The bartender set down our drinks. Emily's was something clear with a lime. Vodka, gin, rum, tonic, soda, 7-Up. Something of that sort. She smelled sweet and syrupy, the way people do after they've been drinking for a long time. But I couldn't exactly smell what kind of booze she was drinking.

I took a sip of my scotch, lit a cigarette, and asked, "What kind of drugs did Madeline do?"

"Everything. Cocaine, a lot. But heroin, too. You know, you get too high you have to find a way to come down."

"Was it pharmaceutical cocaine?"

"You've been to the dentist." She giggled like she'd just made a joke.

"I have."

"She felt bad about that girl who got fired. But she'd stopped using by then and if they found out it was her she'd have lost her license. Her career was important to her. And she had her kids to think about, you know?"

"She wasn't thinking about her kids when she stabbed her husband," I pointed out.

"I don't know what she was thinking about when she did that."

"Was there really a mistress? Was her husband cheating on her?"

She pushed aside the dregs of her last drink and started the new one. "He was, yes."

"Do you know who he was seeing?"

"A girl named Jane. Jane Weeks."

"How do you know? You didn't know Wes. Did Madeline tell you?"

"No. I knew Jane. She's the kind of girl who gets around. She used to go with anyone who'd give her drugs, you know?" I had the feeling that Emily had been one of those anyones in her day.

"How do I find her?"

"I don't know. They came and got her. I don't know where they took her." She took a gulp of her drink; she'd already managed to down half of it.

"Who came and got her?"

"The people who come and get you when you die."

"She's dead? How? How did she die?"

"They found her stabbed to death in her apartment."

I stared at her for a moment. Then guessed, "The same day that Wes Berkson died."

"Yes."

I almost asked her why no one figured this out, but that would have been stupid. Emily wouldn't have known. In fact, I knew more than she did. I'd worked with the CPD. I knew that when a person confessed the investigation consisted of corroborating the confession and little more. No detective would think, "Hey maybe they killed someone else. Someone they're not confessing to." I also knew that a dead junkie was not a high priority. It would likely be labeled a drug deal gone bad. The investigation into her death would have been as superficial as trying to find out who her dealer was, and when that didn't pan out it wouldn't have gone much further.

"Why? Why would Madeline kill them both and then only confess to killing her husband?"

"I don't know. I really don't," Emily said.

Then she asked me to buy her another drink.

Chapter Fourteen

I slept at my office that night rather than go back to Brian's. I felt like we'd all be more comfortable that way. After The Closet, I stopped at a liquor store and bought a pint of cheap scotch and finished it off before trying to sleep. My mind was in overdrive. Why had Madeline done the things she did? From the things people said, she didn't seem the sort to get so worked up over her husband having an affair that she'd kill two people, and yet that seemed to be exactly what she did do. The other thing was that she had known about the affair for some time. She didn't just find out that day. That was a lie. So, why that particular day? And why confess to one murder but not the other? Of course, none of this was going to help Owen get her a reduced sentence. Even in the unlikely event the reason she killed two people made her more sympathetic, explaining that opened her up to another murder charge, another trial and another sentence. None of that was good.

Since I'd left Joseph's priest garb over at Brian's and I needed to shave, at six that morning I dragged my slightly hungover self the four blocks to his apartment. Brian and Franklin were still asleep so I was able to shave, shower and dress without waking them. I dug around Brian's kitchen for a pail, and then rooted around for a piece of paper and a pen to make a sign. From a bakery bag, I made a simple sign that said Support African Orphans. After I taped it to the pail I chuckled. The sign could be read as giving money to feed African orphans; it could also be read as funding a charity devoted to creating them.

Quietly leaving Brian's, I walked back to the Belmont El station then went right by it. I was too hungry to go directly downtown and it was still early. I grabbed the newspaper and went to Ann Sathers. The hostess greeted me with a cheerful and disconcerting, "Good morning, Father." I almost objected but then remembered how I was dressed. Pretending to be a priest was going to take some getting used to.

Over coffee and a delicious cinnamon roll, I read the front page. Khadafy and the Brits were having one of those spats that always result in the wrong people dying. An Arlington Heights man said he was framed in a heroin bust. His story was that a friend wanted to win the release of his wife and brother-in-law so he set-up a sting with the DEA. He claims to have had no knowledge of the drugs in the suitcases he carried as a favor. I thought the whole thing was dubious on all sides, but I did wonder if anyone involved knew Wes Berkson. Standard Oil spilled millions of gallons of oil off the coast of France and now a judge has decided that they had to pay for the damages. What a terrible fate, to actually be responsible for the things you've done.

I put the paper aside and had scrambled eggs with Swedish sausage. I was tempted to order another cinnamon roll. I was still on the thin side so I could risk it. I decided to get one to go and have it later. I wasn't looking forward to the day. Surveillance was the least interesting part of my job and I did my best to never do it. It was very likely a pointless exercise. I didn't expect to find out much of anything, but it was the only thing I could think to do.

While I waited at the cashier in front of the restaurant, one of the other customers put a quarter in my bucket. I smiled and thanked the woman. Then I wondered if I should have said, "Bless you." It was more in character. Saying "bless you" wasn't exactly a sacrament so I wasn't running afoul of my promise to Joseph.

It was almost eight when I arrived at Federal Plaza. People began to arrive for work around that time so it was perfect. I had no idea what the rules were for soliciting donations in public, so I decided to position myself outside the lobby of the Federal Building. The plaza seemed more "public" and might have different rules than the lobby. I studied the flow of workers into the building to decide which door was used most often. On Monday, I'd switch locations to get full coverage. There were entrances on each of the four sides of the lobby. I decided to spend the day positioned on the northeast corner. I could see two entrances from there and I was just a few feet from the entrance to the subway. Anyone who arrived via the El would have to walk right by me. The Calder bird was to my left and I had a decent view of anyone who decided to hang around looking at it.

By eight-thirty I had blessed a lot of people. Most of whom put a quarter or two in my pail. A couple dropped in a dollar bill. A black woman blessed me right back. I worried that someone might ask me more about the charity so I began making up a story in my head. I knew that there was starvation in Africa but to be honest I wasn't exactly sure where. I began thinking of African countries I knew of. The Congo. Nairobi. Ethiopia. British Guiana. I worried that some of the names had changed. I didn't want to tell someone that we were helping orphans in some no-longer existing African country. Or one that wasn't actually suffering famine. If anyone asked, I'd have to say "various African countries." That would be the best way to handle it.

The bucket was already heavy by nine. I wondered if I might need to go to a bank and change the coins for paper at lunchtime. At the rate I was going, my arms were going to be very tired. I decided I'd stick it out until ten o'clock and then take a short break, stretch my legs and maybe put the bucket down for a few minutes.

Around nine-thirty, the two Federal agents I'd ridden in the elevator with crossed the plaza. They didn't come up from the subway, they came around the post office as though from a parking garage somewhere nearby. Neither of them noticed me, which was a relief.

At about quarter to ten my beeper went off. I studied the little black box for a minute and was able to figure out that I didn't recognize the number. That meant it might be a call from my potential landlord. I certainly hoped it was. I clipped my beeper back onto my belt a little self-consciously. I wondered if a priest would even have a beeper. Was I giving myself away?

Fifteen minutes later I went down into the Jackson subway station to use the payphone, eating my extra cinnamon bun on the way. The phone was located on the platform so I had to buy a ticket. Of course it wasn't like I didn't have correct change, though I did get a look from the CTA agent when I took the change directly out of the bucket. There was a train about to leave when I got to the pay phone so I waited until it pulled out. As soon as it was pulling away, I put my quarter in and dialed Mrs. Harker.

"This is Nick. I want to find out how Terry's doing." I said when she picked up.

"He have big appetite." Which told me she already loved having the boy there. Now, I worried that I'd done something terrible to the old lady. Eventually, I was going to have to take him away.

"Listen, I have a beeper now. Let me give you the number."

"You have what?"

"A beeper. A pager."

"I don't know what is."

"I'm going to give you a phone number. Write this down."

I gave her the number and then she asked, "Who is phone?"

"No one. You dial in your number and I'll call you back."

"Is answering machine?"

"Sort of. Except I know exactly when you call."

"What is for?"

"It's for emergency."

"Everything a-okay. We no have trouble."

"Good. But if you do you can call that number and I'll call you right back."

"You come Sunday. You show me."

"Okay, I'll show you on Sunday."

I said goodbye just as another train was coming by. I doubt she heard me. Pulling the pager off my belt, I clicked the button until I got the number that had beeped me. I put in another quarter, resenting the recent hike from a dime, and dialed the number.

"Two Towers," a woman's voice said.

"Is this Clementine?"

"It is."

"This is Nick Nowak," I said, bracing myself for a no.

"Ah, our new tenant."

"Oh great. Can I come by later and get the keys?"

"Of course, I'm here until seven."

"I'll be there by five-thirty."

"See you then."

I left the station and went back to my spot on the plaza. The next two hours were crushingly dull. The number of people going in and out dropped to a trickle between ten-thirty and eleven-thirty, and it seemed that most of the people who walked by had already put a coin or two into my pail.

I tried to think through what I was looking for. Most of the offices above me were government agencies. That meant I'd been staring at government employees all morning. But the informer probably didn't look like a government employee. So, what did the people I'd seen have in common? I couldn't tell yet. That might be because interspersed among the government workers were people who came to deal with the IRS or their Alderman or some other government agency.

Back up, I told myself. I was looking for someone in the Outfit. Someone who was close enough to Jimmy during the period when the crimes were supposedly committed. The crimes noted in the files began in the late sixties. If the informant had been in his mid-twenties he'd be at least in his mid-forties by now. That meant I didn't have to look at anyone under forty. That helped. Also, since the informant was in the Outfit it was not someone black. As far as I knew there were no black members of the Outfit. They had their own crime syndicates. When it came to crime, separate but equal was still the rule and no one was going to go to court and ask for forced integration. So, I could ignore all the black people that walked by me. That right there was about twenty-five percent. Eliminating the under forties meant I could cut out another twenty-five percent. Half the people who walked by, I could ignore.

What else? We were talking about a man. Prince Charles. There was no Princess Di in the files. I was looking for a white man over forty. That cut things down another twenty-five to thirty percent. I could also cut out the suits. White men in their forties and fifties were very likely to be working the higher level government positions. But they were also likely to be wearing nice suits. No one was going to put on a nice suit with a crisp white shirt to come in and inform on a mobster. The few times when I'd seen them in person, or even in the newspaper, members of the Outfit tended to dress like they were about to go shoot a round of golf. They generally opted for a sort of high-class leisurewear. It was an in-your-face way to tell the rest of the world they were too good for hard work. Their lives were like a permanent vacation. With a little violence thrown in. Having a better idea of what I was looking for didn't mean I turned anything up before lunch, but it did make me sure I hadn't let the informant walk by me.

At twelve-thirty I walked over to Cooke, Babcock and Lackerby. When I walked in the receptionist's mouth dropped open. Then I remembered that I was dressed like a priest. I smiled at her and said, "Part time job." That earned me the kind of scowl that could only come from a practicing Catholic. "You have something for me?"

Grudgingly, she handed me a manila envelope. I sat down in one of the comfortable leather chairs, took Wes Berkson's autopsy out of the envelope and read it.

The body is that of a well-developed, well-nourished adult Caucasian male, 134 pounds and 71 inches, whose appearance is appropriate for the stated age of 37 years, it began. I studied the sentence for a moment. One hundred and thirty-four pounds was too little for a man who was nearly six feet tall. I guessed that when the examiner described the corpse as well-nourished he meant during the developmental years. There were no signs of malnourishment during growth. Malnourishment during adulthood would not leave those permanent signs. He went on to describe the body as cold and purple with obvious rigor mortis present. In other words, dead. Then he described the parts of the body he could see. He described them as normal, except for the presence of lesions on one hand and arm and around both ankles. There was no stated reason for the lesions.

For identifying marks, the examiner noted a small surgcal scar in the right lower abdomen at McBurney's point. McBurney's point could have been a yacht club for all I knew, but I did understand a scar in the right lower abdomen probably indicated an appendectomy.

The part of an autopsy that most detectives jump right to is Evidence of Injury. This one began with the words: *Stab wound of the chest*. Then it described the entrance wound as *on the midline chest beneath the sternum, twenty-two inches below the top of the head at the anterior midline.* The wound itself was one and three quarters inches wide. This statement was uncomfortably visual: *Having washed away the blood, no other marks remain on the rest of the chest.* The wound was then described as being five inches deep and angled upwards. The wound track traveled through the soft tissue of the chest, the pericardial sac, and both cardiac ventricles.

Next the examiner looked at Wes' clothing. He described a two inch-slit in a Kiss World Tour T-shirt. He also described the shirt as being completely soaked in blood.

After that, the report went on to examine each organ system. Other than the previously described wound, the heart and major arteries were normal for a man of Wes' age. The respiratory system showed problems. The report described swelling of tissue in both lungs and suggested that it was due to pulmonary edema. I'd have to look that up to see how dangerous it was, but there was at least the possibility that Mrs. Levine was right and Wes had not been long for the world. The other organ systems were within a normal range. There was nothing else out of the ordinary in the report. The conclusions were all things I already knew. He was stabbed. Madeline had done a good job.

Chapter Fifteen

I asked the receptionist if Mr. Lovejoy was available to see me for five minutes. She hit the intercom button on the phone, dialed a single number, and asked Owen if he had a moment. Then she told me to go back. I took my time walking back to his office. I needed the extra few seconds to figure out how to say what I needed to say.

"I found Emily Fante," I said after we finished our hellos.

"Did you?"

"I did." I left a pause. I wasn't quite sure what to say. "It's not helpful. In fact, it's the opposite."

"Tell me."

"Are you sure you want to know?"

"Yes."

"The reason no one could find Wes Berkson's mistress is that she's dead. She was killed the same day as Wes. Earlier. She was stabbed."

"Fuck. I didn't want to know that."

I shrugged an "I told you so."

"You think Madeline killed her?"

"It looks very likely, don't you think?"

"Then why didn't she confess to both murders?"

"Because she knew we'd get here. She could figure out that she'd get less time for one murder than she would for two."

"That's very premeditated."

"She knew for some time that her husband was having an affair. The whole thing was premeditated."

"Then why? Why kill both? Why not just kill the mistress? And why then?"

"I don't know the answer to that."

"I read the autopsy," he said.

"Then you saw it." Meaning the pulmonary edema.

"I did."

"Which raises the question, why kill a dying man?"

"She didn't know that he was dying."

"Her mother suspected. Madeline would have suspected, too."

"None of this is helping," Owen said. "Our job is to make her look like a woman who deserves leniency."

"Maybe you should just put her up there. Skip everyone else. I mean, she orchestrated the whole thing. Let her play it out."

"That's not a bad idea."

"Tell her to cry."

"My thoughts exactly."

I stood there a moment, awkwardly. Since I'd pretended to quit Jimmy's case for the Feds listening in, I was technically done working for Owen. "Um, so I'll send you my invoice. Let me know if you have anything else come up."

"Yes, of course. I'm sure we'll have something soon."

We gave each other a silly smile and then I walked out of his office.

I managed to get back to Federal Plaza before two o'clock by skipping lunch. I watched as the office workers came back from their own lunch. Few of them looked excited to be returning. I did continue to get donations though. The largest came with whiffs of alcohol, as though those who drank their way through lunch were trying to make up for it by giving to charity. I didn't see anyone even close to the parameters I was looking for. I gave some thought to the possibility that I was wrong about the kind of person who might be betraying Jimmy. I just didn't feel wrong.

I let my mind wander onto other things. Did I really want to paint my apartment? It was a lot of trouble. And even though I didn't particular care for the current color, I'd just spent a year in a transient hotel; I was fully capable of ignoring my environment. But that was half the point of the apartment, wasn't it? It was an environment I wouldn't want to ignore. I'd be able to sit at my window, look at the lake, enjoy my coffee in the morning and my scotch in the evening. And if I managed to pick a color and paint the walls, I could enjoy that, too. Isn't that the way normal people thought about things? And wasn't that what I was trying to become?

Around three, a short black woman of about seventy appeared out of no where and attempted to talk me out of my Catholicism. She appreciated that I was following the Lord but I was doing it all wrong. She was particularly distressed by our belief in saints, which she likened to the pantheon of Greek gods. I put up a little bit of a fight, just enough that she didn't tip to the fact that I wasn't really a priest, and then excused myself to take a break. I was starving, so I walked down to Dearborn and Adams and found a lunch counter called Mel's Italian. I ordered a beef sandwich with onions, peppers, and mozzarella cheese. It came with fries and a Coke.

There was something about the Madeline Levine thing that kept nagging at me, except I couldn't figure out exactly what it was. She had to have had a reason for killing two people. And I thought it had to be a better reason than that they were fucking. I just didn't know what that reason was, but the idea that I should know just wouldn't go away. I was missing something. I knew it. But I couldn't think what.

When I went back to my spot on the plaza, I began to wonder how often Prince Charles came in to see the task force. Though it seemed like he'd covered most everything in the transcripts I read, the closer we got to an indictment the more often he'd need to come in. The transcripts covered twelve or fifteen hours of testimony. The testimony Prince Charles would give in front of a Federal Grand Jury would probably be limited to three or four hours. They'd have to do some work to get the important details in.

Around five, I decided to call it a day. People would be leaving work soon but there wasn't any reason to think that Prince Charles would be among them. He was an informant; he wouldn't be keeping regular hours. In fact, I needed to keep that in mind. He was more likely to come in after the rush of people early in the morning and leave before the rush of people on their way home. My bucket was more than half full. I probably had forty or fifty dollars just in change. I had a pocket stuffed with singles. I'd gotten concerned that they'd fly out of the pail when I took my breaks.

I went down into the subway and caught the Jackson/Howard going north. Rush hour had begun and the car I was in was crowded. It was one of the new silver cars with the orange and butterscotch colored seats. A woman in her early sixties got up and tried to give me her seat. I refused, of course, and then a younger man of about twenty-six or so took the hint and got up to give me his seat. I couldn't think of a good reason to refuse him, so I got to sit.

Was Joseph's life full of these little perks? Would he miss this sort of privilege? Or, knowing that he had doubts, did they weigh on him? Did they make him feel guilty? People had been looking at me differently all day. I was very aware of that. Certainly a lot of people just ignored me. Non-Catholics. But a lot of other people silently afforded me respect. Well, they gave respect to the collar I wore. Not me.

I got off the train at Belmont and walked down to Clark and then up to my office. There were no messages on my answering machine and that made me happy. I didn't feel like returning any calls. In fact, I was done with work for the day. I was not going to think about Madeline Levine-Berkson or Jimmy English for the rest of the day. I might try to think of something I could do on Jimmy's case Saturday morning or I might not. I'd decide then. I put the plastic bucket on my desk and dug around until I found a bag of my clothes. I pulled out an old Irish sweater I sometimes wore and put that on instead of Joseph's priestly collar. I figured I'd be warm enough with just the sweater so I skipped my coat. I had an idea about how I wanted that night's "normal" date with Joseph to go, so I tried calling him. After eight rings, he picked up.

I'd barely said hello when he said, "You're cancelling, aren't you?" I couldn't tell if he was disappointed or not.

"No. I just want you to meet me somewhere else." I gave him my new address.

"Where is this?"

"It's a surprise. Do you like surprises?"

"I don't know. I don't think anyone's tried to surprise me since I was in grammar school."

"Okay, well, I guess we'll find out."

I hung up and hurried out of my office. I had a lot to do in the next hour. First, I walked quickly over to Two Towers. Clementine was in the office and, after she answered the buzzer, she asked me to come back and sign the lease. When I finished signing, which took all of a second, she gave me my copy of the lease and my keys.

"Um, I have someone coming by in a bit. Can we get my name on the buzzer?"

"Sure, just give me ten minutes."

Rather than go up the apartment, I hurried out of the building. My first stop was the Walgreen's on Broadway where I, perhaps too optimistically, bought a package of Trojans and a tube of KY jelly. The cashier didn't bat an eye. I'm sure she thought I was just another straight guy trying not to knock up his girlfriend. I wondered if that assumption was soon to change.

Then I walked up Broadway to the Treasure Island at Cornelia. Treasure Island called itself "America's Most European Supermarket" and it was filled with things you couldn't get in other stores. There was a sign at the edge of the parking lot that was designed to look like a treasure map. It was exactly the place I wanted for my "normal" date.

It had taken almost fifteen minutes to walk there so I was rushed as I entered the store. I grabbed a cart and started heading down each aisle. I grabbed a loaf of French bread, a hard salami, two kinds of hard cheese, two bottles of red wine, a cork screw, two wine glasses, and a plastic coated red gingham table cloth. I cringed a little when the cashier told me it was thirty-one dollars and forty cents. We could have had a nice dinner out for that. Still, I liked the idea of my "normal" date and I was going to stick with it. I was definitely running late when I got out of the store, so I grabbed a cab and ignored the cabbie's scowling when he realized it was only a six-block trip.

Unlocking my door and walking into the apartment was a good feeling. The sun was going down and lights were beginning to come on in the buildings I could see along Lake Shore Drive. My electricity was on, it was included in the rent, but there were only three light fixtures. In the bedroom there was a ceiling light, the bathroom had a light and there one in the tiny kitchen. I turned them all on and began spread out my little picnic. I kicked myself for not buying candles, though I didn't have anything to stick them—

The intercom buzzed. I went over and pressed the talk button.

"Hello?" I let go of the button and pressed the listen button.

"Nick?" It was Joseph.

Rather than keep hitting buttons to talk, I pressed the button to let him into the building. I stepped back into the living room to make sure everything was the way I wanted. It looked just fine and the light from the little kitchen was actually plenty. I opened the front door and waited for Joseph to get out of the elevator. A minute or so later he appeared, looking in both directions trying to figure out which way to go. He saw me and I waved. He smiled, showing me his broken tooth. *Why did I like that tooth so much?* I wondered. I led him into the apartment and shut the door. He turned to look at me, questioning, but I pulled him into a kiss.

He pushed me away and asked, "Where am I?"

"This is my new apartment."

"Oh." He looked around again. "I love what you've done with the place."

"I've had the keys for an hour."

"I like it. That's a great view."

"The view got me. If they'd shown me a closet with a lumpy cot and that view I probably would have rented it." And I could have lived on a lumpy cot. Had in a way for a long time. But now the person who'd done that seemed far away. Remote. For just a moment I wondered what I was I doing. Wanting things, the apartment, the man standing next to me, that was danger—

"Hello? Where'd you go?" Joseph asked.

"I'm right here," I said. "Can I offer you a glass of wine?"

"Yes, absolutely."

I picked up the bottle of wine and the corkscrew up off the tablecloth and began the process of getting the wine open.

"How did you find this place?"

"I interviewed someone in the building."

"Oh, will that be awkward? Running into them on laundry day?"

"I don't think so. It wasn't a combative interview."

"Is it expensive?"

"I don't know. It's more than my last apartment by a lot. But I think it's probably less than a lot of what you find on Lake Shore Drive."

He nodded like that mattered somehow.

"I think you'll be very happy here."

"I'm thinking of painting. But I don't know what color. What do you think?" It felt like an important question and I tried not to think about why.

He looked around. "Well the carpet's brown. So it has to be something that goes with brown."

"Doesn't everything go with brown?"

"Yes and no. It's a dark brown so you don't want to pick anything dark because then it might feel like a cave. Why are you asking me? I don't know anything about color."

"You're doing great. And I asked for an opinion. Not a decision."

I'd gotten the bottle of wine open and poured us each a glass. After I handed him his, he raised it and said, "To your new place."

"Thank you."

We drank.

"Nothing too pastel," he said. "You're not an infant."

"Thank you for noticing that."

"Beige," he suggested.

I didn't think I'd like beige, but I said, "That's an idea. I'll have to go to The Great Ace and look at paint."

I offered him some food and we sat down on the floor. Then I realized something rather important. "Shit. I didn't buy a knife." Or a cutting board. Or even a plate. Joseph pulled out his keys. As part of his key chain he had a tiny fold out knife.

"You were a Boy Scout, weren't you?"

"Eagle Scout, yes."

"I only made it to Webelos. Which explains why I'm not prepared."

I didn't bother using the knife on the bread; that ripped apart easily enough. It worked well enough on the cheese, but was practically useless when it came to the salami. It wasn't long before we resorted to simply biting big chunks out of it. Laughing at each other each time we did.

"I hope this is okay to bring up," Joseph began, seeming uncomfortable. "I'm not supposed to mention anything you said in confession. Even if it's just you and me, but...well, since I may be setting all that aside, I'm going to fudge the rule. Are you doing better than you were?"

"Are you asking if I've forgiven myself?"

"I suppose, yes."

"I don't know. I haven't thought about it much."

He smiled. "Not thinking about it is probably a good thing."

"I killed someone and I shouldn't think about it. You want to leave the priesthood and you have to think about it all the time. That doesn't make sense."

"No, it makes sense. You made a decision that can't be undone, there's nothing to think about anymore. I'm about to make a decision that will completely change my life. That needs to be thought through."

"I guess I'm better. I mean things are going better, so I must be."

"It's okay to be happy."

I didn't want to think about that. I wasn't sure I agreed but I also didn't want to challenge him. I wanted to just let it be true. I changed the subject. "Now let me ask you a question. Are you going to miss listening to people's secrets?"

"I wouldn't miss the secrets. People's secrets are much less interesting than you'd think. There's a lot of coveting going on. In fact, that's most of it. A lot of hoping family members die. Rarely does someone have an interesting secret. I do like absolving people though. They seemed so relieved, so pleased. I think I would miss that."

I leaned over and kissed him. He kissed me back for just a brief moment and then pulled away. "I'm not sure I should be doing that."

I nuzzled him. "You can go to confession tomorrow."

"The certainty of absolution should not allow us to sin."

I felt my face set into a scowl. "This is rather silly, don't you think? We both know why you came here."

"I—Nick, if I decide to remain a priest I don't want to have to regret too much."

"So that's a real possibility? Remaining a priest?"

"I made the decision to become a priest, it's possible that I might make the decision to stay one."

"Earlier this week you sounded like thinking things over was just a formality."

"I want my life to mean something. I'm thinking seriously of staying."

"So then what are we doing?"

"Becoming friends. Maybe."

That annoyed me. Mainly because I felt there had been some false advertizing. "The trouble with that is that I've fucked most of my friends. In fact, it's kind of how I make friends."

"Do most gay guys do that?"

"I don't know. I've never done a survey. And besides, what difference does it make. If you're going to stay a priest then you don't need to know anything about gay guys, do you? Except maybe which Bible verses to condemn us with."

"You're angry, aren't you?"

"I wanted to fuck you."

"Is that all?"

"Well, if you were good at it, I'd want to fuck you again."

"You're being rude on purpose. I've hurt your feelings."

I wasn't hurt. He was right the first time, I was angry. Strangely, I felt safe wrapped in my anger. It felt like armor. With as much distain as I could muster, I said, "It'd take a lot more than you to hurt my feelings. It's time for you to go."

Chapter Sixteen

After Joseph left, I had a couple of options. I could sit down and drink the remaining bottle and a half of wine. Or, I could wander out to the bars and see if I could find someone to fuck. Neither option was particularly appealing. I didn't want to drink all that wine because I didn't feel like having a hangover in the morning since I would be going out Saturday night and likely have one on Sunday. Sometimes it's good to plan hangovers in advance. I didn't want to pick some guy up, not because I wasn't horny, but the idea of actually having to talk to someone at that moment was not appealing. I was talked out.

Of course it was Friday night and, as a still almost young gay man living in the city, I should be out having a blast. Instead, I decided I'd move. I had a great parking place on Aldine just around the corner, but I decided it was worth giving up. I could shuttle a lot of my boxes and my clothes from my office to the apartment and be half moved in by midnight. Yeah, it would have made more sense to go out and look at paint to decide on a color and paint the place before I moved in, but after fantasizing that Joseph might help me I wasn't up to doing it on my own.

I was going to be fine. I knew that. The only real upside of having a lot of big shitty things happen to you is that when little shitty things come along they're kind of a breeze. I mean, all Joseph really did was tease me a little. Comparatively, it was not a big deal. And I knew better. All along I knew better. He was a priest. Never try to fuck a priest. Even if they're talking about leaving the priesthood. That should be a rule somewhere. A former priest, maybe. And even then I don't know. The thing is, your big competition is God. And if God wants your boyfriend he's going to take him. Best to avoid the whole thing.

That night I was able to bring three loads of stuff over in my car. Dishes, books, linens, clothes. I felt like I'd accomplished something, which helped to make up for the evening's disappointment. It also meant that I had a pillow and a couple of blankets so I could make myself reasonably comfortable sleeping on the living room floor. Before bed, I opened up one of the director's chairs, put my feet up on the marble windowsill and finished the first bottle of wine while I studied the lights of Lake Shore Drive.

The next morning I woke around eight. I went right to the window to look out. The sun was nowhere to be seen. The sky was a layer of gray clouds that looked like an overused, lumpy mattress bearing down on us. I didn't have a shower curtain, so I took a bath in the shallow tub. I liked the idea of nine bathtubs and bathrooms directly below me. I even liked thinking of all the people nearby in their own little apartments. If you didn't like high rises you could liken them to ant farms. The analogy didn't bother me in the least. In fact, I kind of liked it. Ants are busy. They have too much to do to feel bad.

A half an hour later, I was dressed and eating breakfast at the Melrose. I had the *Daily Herald* in front of me and was reading about the bombing at Heathrow. Twenty-two people were injured but no one was killed. According to the article, no one had taken responsibility for the incident. I couldn't help but remember my date with Joseph and being evacuated from the Broadway. Even with the threat of sudden death, it was a much more fun and much more "normal" a date than the one we'd had the night before. I told myself to stop thinking about it, and began to plan my day over bacon and eggs.

I needed to write my final reports for the Levine case and prepare my invoice. Something still nagged at me about the whole thing, so maybe I'd figure out what it was when I went back and summarized everything I did. But would it make a difference? That was the real question. *What could make a difference for Madeline at this point?* I wondered. I also wanted to do something more on Jimmy's case. Although, what that was, I wasn't entirely sure.

There were three messages waiting for me on my answering machine. Two were from Brian wondering where I was. That was a little shitty, I supposed. I'd just disappeared for the last two days. The third message was Joseph. Calling to say he was sorry. Again. I deleted his message before he was completely finished. Fuck him.

I got out my Smith Corona and typed out the reports on the Levine case. Unfortunately, no great revelation came to me. It took about an hour and a half, but I finished the reports, took them downstairs to make copies, and then put them in a manila envelop that I would deliver to Owen on Monday morning.

After that, I got out a pad and started thinking about Jimmy's case. The files focused on the Perelli murders but they also contained information on Jimmy's other operations. In interviews, restaurant owners described being shaken down by a bagman named Mickey Troccoli. I knew that name. He used to pick up a monthly payment from Davey Edwards when Paradise Isle was still in business. Following Mickey's trail was what led me to Jimmy in the first place. It would be worth talking to Mickey. He might know something.

On the pad, I made the note: FIND MICKEY TROCCOLI. A quick glance at the phonebook told me he wasn't going to be all that easy to find. I might need to go down to the main library and do a newspaper search. If Mickey had ever been arrested there would be an address in the newspaper.

Then I backtracked. If the Feds arrested Jimmy on the Perelli murders, one of the things the defense would want to do is show that others had motive to kill the couple. Better yet, that others had a more compelling motive to kill them than Jimmy did. I needed to look into the Perellis themselves. It wouldn't be a bad idea to talk to any remaining family members. I dug through the files until I found the police report on the Perelli murders. I figured it would have a lot of what I wanted. The report listed the Perelli's address as Snowberry Court in Downer's Grove. I assumed it wasn't far from the restaurant parking lot where they were found. I took a chance and cracked open the phonebook again.

None of the current crop of eleven Perellis lived on Snowberry Court. In fact, none of them lived in Downer's Grove. That didn't mean some or all of them weren't related to the Perillis, it just meant I didn't score a bull's-eye. I went back to the report and looked around until I found Josette Perelli's maiden name: Delorte. I returned to the trusty phonebook and checked out all the Delortes. Now I scored a bull's-eye. There was a Delorte on Snowberry Court. N. Delorte. I went ahead and dialed.

A woman answered the phone. She sounded mature. Like she'd been on Social Security since it was invented. "Is this Mrs. Delorte?"

"Yes. Yes, it is. Who is this?"

"I'm an old friend of Shady Perelli's."

"No you're not. Shady didn't have any friends."

"Well, actually I was a friend of Josette's."

"That's more likely. She had friends. She had lots of friends." The woman didn't make it sound like a good thing. "That was the kind of girl she was."

"I'd like to come out and ask you some questions. Is there a time that's good?"

"Never. That would be a good time."

"All right. Then why don't we just talk a little now?"

"I can hang up any time I want to."

"And I can't stop you, can I? So are you Josette's mother?"

"You knew that already."

I didn't, but why correct her? "Are you serious when you say that Shady didn't have any friends?"

"His name was Shady. Don't you think he earned it?"

"Lots of shady people have friends though."

"He was shady and he had a loud mouth. If you were friends with him he stabbed you in the back and then told everyone your secrets." That sounded like an opinion she'd held for a long time and was glad for the chance of airing.

"What did your daughter see in him?"

"Lord knows. He wasn't even a good-looking man. But don't think she didn't give as good as he gave. My girl was a pistol. Could have any man she wanted, and did."

That opened up a whole new can of worms. Were the Perelli murders even related to the Outfit? "Why do think they were killed, Mrs. Berkson?"

"Shady was talking to someone. The cops. The FBI. I don't know who."

"Who was he talking about?"

"Doves, who else?"

Doves was the man at the top of the heap, and had been for a very long time. He was Jimmy's boss. His name was mentioned a few times in the files, but mostly in questions. The Feds would ask about him, but Prince Charles would claim they weren't acquainted. He wasn't implicated in any crime. Which made me wonder if the Perelli murder was something that Doves orchestrated and was now being blamed on Jimmy. Was Doves behind the whole thing? Was he pulling the strings at the task force? Hey, it was Chicago. Stranger things had happened.

"But nothing happened to Doves," I said. "There were no charges filed."

"No. Because Shady died."

"Why kill them both, though?"

"I told you, my girl had friends. Well, Shady got tired of her having friends. Wouldn't let her out of his sight."

"So if she hadn't been there…"

"Exactly. I'm gonna hang up now. I got something on the stove."

I doubted she had something on the stove but she hung up before I could say so.

I went back to worrying about how I might find Mickey Troccoli. *What did I know about him?* He was low level Outfit. He worked for Jimmy. That meant Jimmy could probably tell me how to reach him. But did I want Jimmy to know I was looking for him? No. I didn't. I didn't have any evidence that Mickey was the informant. None at all. And I didn't want Jimmy thinking that I might. I didn't want him "persuading" anyone who didn't deserve to be "persuaded."

Did I know anything else about Mickey? I had the feeling I did. I vaguely remembered Ross saying something about him. Did he say that Mickey had made a pass at him? He might have. It had been more than three years. I couldn't be completely sure. But what if Mickey Troccoli were gay. Where would I find a gay mobster? It wasn't like there was a specific bar where gay mobsters hung out. Or at least not one I knew about.

The only thing I knew about Mickey was that he went around to bars collecting money once a month. I was going to have to go around to the bars and ask about him. Maybe I could find another bartender who Mickey hit on. One who'd taken him up on the offer; one who might know where he lives.

It was time for lunch. I was supposed to take Sugar to the Glory Hole that night but I had no idea what time. I put in a quick call to her.

"I've been elected to be your escort this evening."

"Oh you have? Well, what time are you picking me up?"

"Actually, I'm hoping to meet you there. I've got some other stops I need to make."

"Well, what kind of escort are you if you're not going to escort me?"

"A shitty one, I guess."

That made her laugh. "I will be there at eight o'clock sharp. I will sit in my car for ten minutes. If you do not come out and escort me inside I will leave. Do you understand me, Mr. Nowak?"

I told her I did and promised I'd be there.

I went to the Golden Nugget for a grilled ham and cheese with some French fries. I ordered a glass of milk to go with it. I was going to be drinking a lot that afternoon, so I wanted to line my stomach. It might be an old wives' tale but it was worth a try. They had the bar rags sitting in a stack by the entrance. I picked up a copy of *Gay Times* and flipped back to their list of bars while I ate. The list was two columns in very small print covering a whole page. It looked exhausting. I bummed a pen off the waitress and crossed off the gay bars out in the suburbs. Then the ones that were up north near Evanston.

From going through the Operation Tea and Crumpets files I had a strong sense of the area Jimmy controlled. As far as gay bars were concerned, there were the bars in Boystown and a bunch of older bars down in

Old Town. I figured I'd hit the bars in Boystown during the afternoon, go home to change my clothes, then head down to the Glory Hole which was on Wells in Old Town. I'd escort Sugar for an hour or two and then I'd hit some of the other bars down that way. I was going to have to limit myself to ordering beers and only drink a half of each one. It's not that I couldn't walk into each of the bars, ask my question, and walk out without getting a drink; it's just that bartenders tend to be friendlier if you present yourself as a customer and tip them first.

I mapped out a route that was going to have me wandering around the neighborhood for most of the afternoon. I kept my money at Mid Town Bank. They had a branch in a small brick building on Broadway south of Barry. I walked down and had the teller give me fifty dollars. That should cover the cost of my afternoon and evening. Technically, I could ask every single bartender for a receipt and get reimbursed with my invoice, but that seemed kind of petty. I was being paid well; I didn't need to nickel-and-dime anyone.

Cutting over to Clark there were three bars in close proximity, the furthest below Diversey: The Limited, Cheeks, and Thumbs Up. All three were small, narrow storefront bars, and each was sleazy in it's own unique way. Of course, I was no stranger to sleazy having wasted a year of my life working at Irving's "L" Lounge.

At Cheeks they were getting ready for a Mr. Cheeks contest. The bar was more populated than you'd expect on a Saturday afternoon. I ordered a Miller and took a couple of sips before I asked the bartender—whose chest was so rock hard and covered in hair that I don't know whether I ever looked up at his face—if he knew Mickey Troccoli.

"I don't learn people's names, man." The way he said it suggested he knew who Mickey was and didn't want to tell me anything about him.

"I'm just asking because I owe him some money and I haven't been able to find him."

"If you want I can get you an envelope and you can put the money in there. If someone named Mickey comes in we'll give it to him." I think he was only half joking. If I'd been able to look up at his face I might have been able to figure it out.

"Thanks. I'll keep looking for him."

My luck wasn't any better at the other two bars down that way. I walked back up to Belmont and hit a trendy place called Dresden. Two doors down from the El, the bar was two storefronts that had been combined. One half was the bar and a couple of tables. The other half was a generously sized dance floor. The place was not a disco like Paradise Isle. It was more new wave and had a rough, homemade feel to it. The way the name was painted onto the front of the building, with is letters hand drawn and bouncing all over the place, and then again the same logo over the bar, put me in mind of the "Life in Hell" cartoons they stuck in the back of the *Reader*. And yet there was also something about the place that seemed to announce they didn't follow trends, they began them.

The bartender there was a scrawny little guy whose very blandness seemed to reject the worked-out and artfully displayed bartenders I was used to seeing in gay clubs. This guy would never have worked at Paradise Isle. I had the feeling if he took his shirt off, customers would ask him to put it back on. I ordered my beer and when he set in front of me, I asked, "Do you know a guy named Mickey Troccoli."

"Who are you? Are you an investigator?"

"I'm a *private* investigator. Nick Nowak. I'd like to talk to Mickey."

His eyes got a little wild and he said, "Shit."

"Why shit?"

"You're a friend of Mickey's."

"No." I decided not to elaborate and see what he said.

"When you walked in, I was hoping you were from liquor control. I filed a complaint. A year ago, for Christ's sake. Far as I know they haven't done a fucking thing. Mickey Troccoli's still coming around."

"Ah. You want to do this on the up and up."

"My business plan is pretty tight. I don't have room for the kind of money they're trying to squeeze out of us." He reached under the bar and pulled out a stack of cocktail napkins. They were thin, barely white and the name of the bar was blurred. He reached out and slid down a stack that was sitting on the bar. These were plump, bright white and the name Dresden fairly jumped off them.

He pointed at the first stack. "These, these shitty ones, they cost ten times what the nice ones cost. But you have to buy the shitty ones. They don't take no for an answer."

"How often does Mickey come in here?"

"I've told him I'm not ordering any more crap from him. So he's here two, three times a week."

"Any pattern to it?"

"Afternoons. During the week. He doesn't like to come in when we're busy."

That didn't work. My weekday afternoons were already taken up by staking out the Federal Plaza.

He studied me for a moment. "I couldn't pay you to make Mickey go away, could I?"

"Not for any amount of money."

"Shit."

"My suggestion...raise your drink prices a quarter and pay him. Life will be easier that way."

Chapter Seventeen

When I stumbled into the Glory Hole, "Thriller" was playing. That seemed appropriate to me since I'd seen the video that went with "Thriller" and Jackson looked to be wearing about as much makeup as your average drag queen. I didn't see Sugar's limo anywhere on the street, so I was on time.

I'd been to six other bars without much luck. Then I'd gone home and done my best to piss out all the beer I'd drunk, taken a cold shower, and then poured myself into a cab. I couldn't stand any more beer, so when I got to the bar I ordered a Johnnie Walker Red on the rocks. It would either straighten me out or kill me. While the bartender poured my drink, I asked if he knew Mickey Troccoli.

"Yeah, Mickey comes in here. Why?"

"I'm looking for him."

"Why?"

"I want to talk to him."

This earned me a dubious look. "He's sort of a scary guy, you know."

"I don't look like I can take care of myself?"

"At the moment you look like you can barely stand up."

"I'm fine. It's just been a busy day."

He set the drink down in front of me and said, "Take your time with this one. You're here to relax, there's no reason to hurry."

I decided I needed to look more sober, so I took a spot by the front window and stood very, very still. If I didn't move, no one would know how drunk I was. Why was I so drunk? I'd only had five beers total. Ten bars, a half beer in each, five beers. Well, no that's not right. I had a scotch at the last bar because the beer was bloating me. And the beer was bloating me because I'd actually finished one or two of them even though I'd planned to have only half a beer at each stop. I wondered if I should go into the bathroom and put my finger down my throat. Strangely, that was not an appealing idea.

I looked around. It was another storefront bar. I was beginning to mix them all up. Like most of the others, the bar at the Glory Hole was against one wall. It was long, stretching almost the entire length of the place. On the opposite wall were some tall tables with stools. There really wasn't another way to arrange one of these places. The bar was half full; barstools full of regulars and most of the tables still open. I wondered where exactly Sugar Pills was going to perform. The only thing even remotely resembling a stage was the bar itself.

I'd taken three sips of my drink when a limousine stopped in front. I was halfway out the door when Brian and Franklin got out of it. That was curious, they'd said they weren't coming. Before I had much time to think about that, Sugar got out of the limo. I almost burst out laughing. Okay, I did burst out laughing, but I was still inside so she didn't hear me. Sugar Pilson had decided to out drag a drag queen. She wore a red dress with puffed shoulders that would put Alexis Carrington to shame. Her hair was up and twisted into a giant, foot-tall bun, her eyelashes were at least two inches long, and her make-up a quarter-inch thick. She looked like a cartoon version of herself, which was completely deliberate.

I held open the door to the bar as they walked in. Brian gave me a frosty hello, while Franklin ignored me completely. Sugar rested a hand on my chest and said, "Don't I look fabulous!"

"Sugar, you look amazing."

Sugar Pilson was originally from Texas. Not the oil part of Texas, the dusty, tarpaper shack part of Texas. The official story is that she was a cheerleader for the Houston Oilers when she met one of the older Pilsons—who may or may not have been a minority owner of the team— promptly married him and then a year later just as promptly divorced him. There are problems with the story. For one thing, there are rumors that she was never a cheerleader, though with her almost naturally blonde hair and perky figure she certainly looked the part. And, for another, there's her divorce settlement. The Pilsons gave her far more money than necessary for a one-year marriage. Even in a community property state, which Illinois was not, she would have received a nice settlement that would have kept her for years in a modest condo close to Evanston if she was careful. Instead, she had a three-story home in the most expensive part of Chicago, a car and driver, a condo in Florida for those days when winter was just too dreary, and enough ready cash to devote most of her time to giving it away. Obviously, she knew something about the Pilsons they did not want known, and not just something embarrassing, something potentially devastating.

Brian and Franklin picked out a table and, before I could offer, went to get a round of drinks.

"You'll find this interesting," Sugar said leaning close. "Since I shifted so much of my charitable giving over to fighting AIDS, Gloria Silver won't write a word about me for her column."

"That's not true," I said, trying not to slur. "There was that blind item she did. 'What cheerleader cum socialite is not recalled at all by her former teammates?' That wasn't about you?"

"It's not. This may come as a surprise to you but Chicago is full of former cheerleaders. Most of whom lie about their ages, making teammates hard to come by."

There was a little edge to her voice, so I said, "Sugar I don't care where you came from. You're all right by me no matter what."

"And that is the sign of a true gentleman."

Brian and Franklin came back with a bottle of champagne and three glasses.

"This is the best they have Sugar. It's nowhere near as good as the bottle we had in the car," Franklin fawned. "That was amazing."

"Darling there's a theory about wine. A very important theory. You always serve the best bottle first when the palate is fresh. The second bottle can be good but need not be too good. The palate has begun to tire.

The third bottle can be rotgut. No one can taste it at that point so why waste good wine on people who can't taste?"

Franklin smiled in a way that was brittle and forced. She was disappointing him, I could tell. He wanted her to be all excess; the best of everything around the clock. And she wasn't. She was a good-humored woman with a strong will and a lot of money that she liked to put to good use.

Brian tugged on my arm and whispered, "Where have you been?"

"I'm sorry. I owe you an apology."

"I was worried. You don't have the safest job in the world."

"I rented an apartment."

"Really? You didn't have to do that."

"Yes I did. If I spent much more time sleeping on your sofa I'd have permanent damage to my spine."

Franklin asked Sugar how much time she spent in Europe each year. "I went to Europe on my honeymoon. I don't think we met a single person who wasn't rude. I can't think of any reason to go back."

Brian pulled me a few feet away. "It's because of Franklin isn't it?"

"He's not my favorite person in the world, but he seems to like you. I don't want to fuck that up."

"I don't know."

"What?"

"I know he likes me but…I have the feeling that if I get sick, he'll leave me."

My heart bounced painfully when he said that. "Are you sick? Do you feel okay?"

"Yeah, I feel fine but you know…it could happen any day. Right?"

"You don't know him well enough to know what he'll do. Sometimes people surprise you." I didn't want to say it, but Ross surprised us both. And Harker certainly surprised me. And not in good ways. One of us was due for a good surprise.

"I'm not sure I want to take that kind of chance." He frowned at me again. "I feel like I've screwed everything up."

"You haven't screwed anything up. I was always going to move out. I'm right around the corner. You can help me paint if you want."

"You're going to paint the apartment?"

"Yeah, it's that ugly white they always paint apartments."

"What color?"

"I don't know. Not beige."

"No. Beige is ugly."

Franklin walked over. "What are we talking about?"

"The ugliness of beige," I told him.

"I love beige. It's so warm." The look on his face said he didn't believe us and with good reason; no one needed privacy to talk about beige.

"Nick got an apartment."

"Congratulations." I think it was the first time he'd ever smiled at me.

"Where did Sugar go?" I asked, just noting her absence.

"Ladies room."

I suspected she was going to be a while in that dress. Unless she was just "powdering" her nose. It was the kind of night that invited that sort of thing.

"Nick's going to paint his apartment. That's why we were talking about beige," Brian said.

This was the moment most friends would volunteer to help. I hoped Brian wouldn't say anything about helping since that might force Franklin into doing the same and there was no way I wanted to spend that much time with him. Quickly, I said, "I'm trying to pick a color. I have no idea how to do that."

"Go with beige," Franklin said dryly. Then turned to Brian and said, "Sugar is amazing. How do you know her?"

That made my stomach queasier than the booze. Brian had met Sugar at Harker's funeral. Fortunately, he just said, "I met her through Nick," and didn't elaborate. Franklin didn't like that answer, though. Too much of Brian's life came back to me.

"Well, she's just terrific."

"She is," Brian agreed. Though I had the feeling they had different definitions of terrific.

I stepped back over to the table so I could set down my glass and light a cigarette. Brian and Franklin said a few things I couldn't hear. Just then Marilyn Monroe came out of the back and one of the guys at the bar held her hand while she climbed a set of plywood steps to get onto the bar. She was a very tall Marilyn and her wig nearly touched the ceiling as she undulated across the bar. The bartender handed her a microphone, which she tapped with a press-on nail to make sure it was working. It was.

When she reached the middle of the bar, she stopped and said, "Good Evening Ladies and Gentleman. My name is Norma Jean Faker. And I want to welcome you all to Glory Hole. We have a wonderful show for you tonight with some of Chicago's most glamorous glamour girls here to entertain you. Starting with… moi!" She waved at someone in the back and said, "Hit it maestro!"

There was a semi-dramatic pause while we waited for the music to start. When it finally did it took just a moment to recognize that it was the real Marilyn singing something I'd never heard before, the chorus of which was "Every Baby Needs a Da-Da-Daddy," so maybe that was the name of it. The recording was crackly and old but it was clearly her. Norma Jean did a good job of faking her way through it. Just then, I noticed someone I knew walking in. He was short, thick, and had the most remarkable eyes. His name was Bobby Martin and I fucked him a very long time ago. Back then, he had floppy hair that he let dip over one eye. Now his hair was clipped close and he looked a little tired. Like he was up after his bedtime even though it couldn't be past nine o'clock.

I excused myself and walked over to him. "Hey Bobby. How you doing?"

"Oh hello! Nice to see you, Nate!"

"Nick." He knew my name. He was just letting me know he was annoyed with me, though I couldn't remember why.

"Nick, that's right. How've you been? I've been terrific. My life is amazing."

"So you're still acting?" People liked you better if you remembered things about them. Though I didn't want to admit to myself why I wanted to be nice to Bobby.

"Well, no. You can't be gay and be an actor. Not in this city. I tried doing commercial work but there are really only two big casting directors. One is a fat old woman who tries to fuck all the pretty young boys. So I'm out of luck there. I don't even fuck attractive women. And the other is an awful cunt who gives you thirty whole seconds, and if you make even the tiniest mistake she'll never see you again."

"I thought you preferred the theater anyway?"

"Ugh! You've never seen bad behavior until you've worked with people who aren't getting paid. When there's no money involved it's all about ego, ego, ego, and when it's all about ego someone is bound to turn into a monster."

"So what's so great about your life if you gave up your dreams?"

"Money. I'm making it hand over fist. I'm like this WordStar Wiz. I'm going from company to company giving classes. What I used to make in a week, I make every single day. Who needs dreams when you can have money?"

"That's one way to look at it."

"Has Sugar Pills been on yet? She'll murder me if I'm late!" He laughed realizing what he'd just said. "Ha! And then you can investigate. Who's that woman in the red dress? She looks like the real Sugar Pilson. But she couldn't possibly be. Are you going to buy me a drink or are you just going to stand there?"

"You're the one with money, why aren't you buying me a drink?" He just rolled his eyes at me until I laughed. "All right, what do you want to drink?"

"Oh...get me a greyhound."

I walked over to the bar and ordered the drink. I didn't order one for myself. I didn't need it. Apparently, fucking Bobby again was a forgone conclusion so I might want to sober up a bit. On second thought, I ordered a Coke. The caffeine might help.

When I brought the drinks back to Bobby, he said, "Freddie's not well. He has KS."

"What's KS?" I had the feeling I knew but didn't know.

"Karposi's Sarcoma," he said, pronouncing it carefully and correctly. I did know what it was. I'd read about it. Brian had talked about it. I was pretty sure I'd seen it on Ross' neck. I couldn't help but think how discomforting it was that people like Bobby were suddenly speaking with the authority of doctors about things they didn't understand three years ago.

"I don't think he's going to make it much longer. You should come see him. He remembers you fondly." I'd fucked Freddie once and, if I recalled correctly, it *was* a memorable experience. But I didn't see how that might require a deathbed goodbye.

Norma Jean Faker had finished her song and done a little monologue. Now she was working up to introduce another drag queen. "And now, one of my favorite ladies. One who's never afraid to tackle a *weighty* issue. The corpulent Cora Copious." Norma Jean Faker scurried off the stage and down the steps. Up came an overweight man in a dress. His outfit was mediocre. More like a toga than a gown. He'd stuck wax fruit all over it. When he got to center stage he pulled a couple of Twinkies out of his bosom and tossed them out to the audience. "I love Twinkies. And the snack cake's not bad either."

He waved a fat hand in the direction of whoever was turning the tape player on and off, and his song began. He lip synched to "I'm Just a Girl Who Can't Say No," which was from some musical I couldn't think of. If Joseph were there I would have asked him.

As her song began, Cora Copious pulled a banana out of her bosom—making me wonder what else was down there—and ate it during her song. Well, first she made suggestive moves with it. Then she ate it.

I had no choice but to bring Bobby back over to my friends. I wasn't ready to leave with him and I certainly didn't want to spend the rest of the evening talking to him, so it was my best option. They were only paying a little attention to Cora Copious.

Sugar was saying, "It's important that the message gets out to everyone. It's not just about gay men. Straight people are starting to get it. Haitians. Drug addicts."

"But they're not the kind of straight people Middle America cares about. I mean, if the cast of *Happy Days* came down with it people might care," Brian said.

"I think you're underestimating people," Franklin disagreed. "People are basically good."

"That is absolutely true," I said. "The problem is that the word good means different things to different people. For some people killing you in the street is good."

"That is so extreme," Franklin said. "I hate it when gays act like we're being attacked in the streets on a daily basis."

My blood pressure spiked. "I've actually been attacked on the street. With my ex. He was badly hurt."

Franklin paled. "I'm sorry. My point wasn't that it didn't happen. I meant that it didn't happen as often as they'd like—"

Bobby interrupted him, "I know at least four people who've been bashed."

"I know people too," Brian said.

Fortunately for Franklin, Cora Copious' song ended and we all had to applaud her. Norma Jean Faker jumped back on stage the minute Cora got down, and announced, "And now ladies and gentlemen, it is my great pleasure to announce the diva herself, Sugar Pills!"

Sugar Pills' real name was Phil Camora. When he wasn't in drag he was a tall, slender, over-plucked young man with brown hair. Forgettable, in a word. Which might be part of why he liked to put on a dress and a wig. When he climbed onto the bar he was wearing a royal blue dress with a huge skirt and a bodice that wrapped around this bare shoulders like a tortilla. He had a large black purse hanging on one arm. As soon as he was fully on the bar, he opened the purse and began dropping fake money on the patrons. The real Sugar let out a huge guffaw that drew Sugar Pills attention. He squinted out into the audience. When he saw Sugar he squealed. "It's you, darling! I can't believe it! I'm so happy I could write a check! Who should I make it out to?"

"Howard Brown Clinic!" Sugar yelled out the name of her new favorite charity.

"You got it babe. Just as soon as I marry again. My bank account is running on empty, so let me tell you the kind of man I'm looking for. I'm looking for a daddy." This was apparently a cue because her music began. The thing that made Sugar Pills stand out was that she sang for herself. She didn't lip synch. The recorded music began, but it was just instrumental. She began to sing about the daddy she wanted, and the lyrics made it clear that her daddy would buy her just about anything. She was good, too. When the song was over she made a few more jokes about how much money Sugar had and then left the stage, bar, whatever.

Sugar Pills didn't even wait for Norma Jean Faker to bring the show to a close, moments after he left the stage he was hurrying toward our little group with one of those funky disc cameras.

"Oh my God, it's absolutely fabulous that you came, darling. Can I get a picture?"

"Of course," Sugar replied. "If you promise to send a copy to Gloria Silver at the *Daily Herald*."

"Will I!" Sugar Pills gasped. "What a girl wouldn't do for a little publicity."

"Oh she won't print it. It's my way of saying 'fuck you.'"

"You want me to say 'fuck you' to the most powerful gossip columnist in Chicago." His eyes glinted for a moment. "Sure, why not? For you, anything."

He handed the camera to Bobby who was already in a snit. "Hello!" Bobby said since he'd barely been acknowledged.

"Hello. I love you. Shut up and take the picture," Phil said in rapid fire. Bobby frowned but complied while the two Sugars posed. After the flash went off, Sugar Pills turned to Sugar Pilson and said, "Now, make me a happy woman and tell me you know the lyrics to 'Sisters' from *White Christmas*."

"I wouldn't say I *know* the lyrics. But I have seen the movie three or four times."

"Oh my God, we have to. There's another show in an hour. You have to do that number with me. We'll lip sync it, don't worry."

"I couldn't."

"Of course you could."

"She said she didn't want to," Franklin said.

"A lady just wants to be coaxed," Sugar Pills said. "Oh my God, we should put together an act and go on the road. Pills and Pilson."

"Pilson and Pills," volleyed the real Sugar.

The negotiations continued. Someone tapped me on the shoulder I turned around and looked at a guy I hadn't noticed before. He was kind of cute.

"I'm Mickey Troccoli. You're looking for me?"

Chapter Eighteen

Mickey Troccoli was not what I was expecting. He was about five foot eight, with a thick chest and a narrow waist, dark brown hair, absolutely straight and parted in the middle, while his eyes were the color of rich, fertile soil and rimmed by thick eyelashes. A mustache gave him a '70s clone look, one that most guys were now trying to avoid, but Mickey was embracing it in a way that almost made it cool. He wore a very tight black T-shirt, Levi's, a jean jacket and motorcycle boots.

"Yes, I am looking for you," I said, leading him away from our group. I had no idea how this was going to go down.

"Why the fuck are you looking for me? I don't know you."

"I'm working for Jimmy English," I told him. "I need to ask you some questions."

"Who are you?"

"Nick Nowak."

"I work for Jimmy but I never heard of you."

"I'm a private investigator. I work with Jimmy's attorneys."

He chewed that over. I doubted he even knew the names of Jimmy's attorneys. I decided to start asking my questions. "There's a task force trying to take Jimmy down. Have you heard anything about that?"

"Of course I have. Who hasn't?"

"Have they tried to talk to you?" If they had it wasn't in the files I was given. But then, unproductive interviews might not be.

"Yeah, they picked me up. Tried to push me around."

"Push you around how?"

"They kept asking me about this Perelli guy who got murdered. I never heard of him but they kept saying I knew him, that I knew what happened to him, that I was there. That was the best, that I was there." Alcohol was clogging my brain so I didn't really know what he meant. Fortunately, he kept talking. "Finally, I said, 'Tell me about this guy Perelli. Where was he murdered? When was he murdered?' Come to find out he was murdered in nineteen seventy-two. Fuck them. In nineteen seventy-two I was seventeen years old. I was trying to pass fucking algebra. I mean, what do they think? That I skipped out on my homework to go whack some guy I never heard of?"

"They probably do think that. Catching a high school assassin would make their day."

"Thing is, I'm nobody, and I want to stay nobody. I work part-time for Jimmy, that's all. I pick up money at this bar, at that restaurant. Yeah, somebody doesn't want to pay I make a few threats, mostly that I'm gonna call Jimmy. They still don't pay; I go ahead and call Jimmy.

He sends someone else to take care of it. I don't know from nothing."

"So you don't have any ambitions in the Outfit?"

"Shit. I didn't even know I was in the Outfit until the Feds told me. I run my uncle's video store. He's got three of them. Drive-In Video. We got drive through windows like you're at the bank. You heard of them?"

"No, I haven't."

"Well, you will. I'm saving up to open up one of my own." He gave me a long, simmering look. "You got more questions?"

"No, I think that covers it. Thanks."

I started to walk back to my friends. Quickly, he said, "I got a question."

"Okay. What is it?"

He looked from side to side like he was going to tell me a secret. "You wanna fuck?"

"Sure, why not?" I said, quickly. The mental arithmetic was easy. I could fuck this sexy little mobster or I could fuck Bobby Martin who probably wouldn't even bother to stop talking while I was doing it.

"You're not too drunk are you?" Mickey asked.

"No. I'm fine." Okay, I had no idea if I was too drunk. But I wasn't going to say, "Yeah, never mind."

We left the bar. I didn't bother to say goodbye to anyone. Didn't bother to tell Bobby there'd been a change of plans. Out on the street, I asked, "You have a car?"

"Of course, I have a car. What kind of a mook do you think I am?"

"I don't know. I guess I'll find out."

He frowned at me and led me over to a brand new Camaro. It was white, with two red stripes down the hood, and a T-bar roof. Mickey noticed me looking the car over. "It's a little loud, but I like it."

I chuckled. "You should see my car."

"Yeah? What you got?"

"It's a Nova. Lime green. Black stripes. Mag Wheels."

He nodded approvingly. "All right."

When we got settled in the low-slung bucket seats, Mickey said, "We gotta go to your place."

"Why? Do you live with your parents?"

"What's it to you? It saves me a lot of money, okay?"

"Hey, it's no big deal. Lots of guys live with their parents." That wasn't exactly true in my experience, but it seemed like a good thing to say.

"I don't give a fuck what you think," he said, suddenly sullen. His pride was wounded and I liked him better for it.

"I live on Lake Shore Drive just above Belmont."

"Ritzy," he said as he did a U-turn on Wells and got us headed north.

"I think it's actually one of the cheapest buildings south of Evanston."

"Okay, not ritzy."

"I just moved in."

The drive was about twenty blocks. I tried to figure out how many miles that might be, but alcohol and math don't mix. Parking on Lake Shore Drive is crazy tight, so we drove around the block a couple of times.

Mickey told me to, "Pray to Parkella"

"Who?"

"Parkella the Goddess of parking."

"Oh. Sure." I tried to look like I might be praying which is about as close to praying as I came anymore. "You're not Catholic?"

"Of course I'm Catholic."

"Then you should be praying to Mother Cabrini."

"Who's that? She live in the projects?"

To be honest, I only remembered her because of Cabrini-Green. "No, she's dead. She's the saint who finds you parking spaces."

"Not if Parkella finds me one first." A minute or so later, he said, "Here we go." And began to parallel park. "It never fails. Parkella always come through."

Quickly, we walked up to my building. It was still a new experience to pull out my keys and open the door from the outer lobby to the inner lobby. I wondered how often I'd be doing it with a virtual stranger in tow, then thought, *If they're all as sexy as Mickey, hopefully often.* In the elevator, I turned to give him a smile and he pulled me down for a kiss. It was sweet and wet. As soon as we got into the apartment he looked around. "There's no bed?"

"It was worn out. I'm going to use my sofa bed for a while."

"Yeah. Where's the sofa bed?"

"It's not here yet."

"No kidding."

"I just moved in yesterday."

"So we're going to fuck on the floor?" He seemed a little offended by the idea.

"Is that a first for you?"

"I'm not a whore."

That made me laugh.

"What the fuck is funny?"

"Talking to you is like adding two and two and getting five."

He eyed me for a long time. I'm not so sure he wasn't doing some math in his head to figure out if two and two did really make five. "That doesn't sound like a compliment," he finally said.

"It's more an observation."

"This is the kind of situation where compliments help."

"Turn around," I told him.

He did. He was facing the lake so it was natural to say, "Nice view."

"Drop your pants."

He looked over his shoulder at me and then undid his belt. His jeans dropped to the floor. Underneath, he wore a pair of red Jockey shorts with a white waistband.

"And the underwear, too."

Bending over, he pulled his underwear down. When he stood back up his T-shirt partly covered his ass.

"Lift up your shirt."

His ass was ample and round, sitting on thick thighs. "That's what I thought," I said.

"What did you think?"

"That you have a nice ass."

"I know I have a nice ass."

"You wanted compliments. That's a compliment. You have a nice ass. You have a very nice ass."

"Yeah, what about the rest of me?"

"The rest of you goes well with your ass."

He broke out laughing. "So it's like that, huh?"

"Like what?"

"Like, you wanna fuck me."

"Isn't that why you came here?"

"I don't know. Maybe I thought I'd fuck you."

I stepped over to him and pushed my hips up to his naked ass. And said, "Yeah. Maybe not." My dick was getting hard and through my jeans I pushed it between the firm cheeks of his ass. I hoped this wasn't going to be an issue. Then he arched his back and ground into me. I figured I could relax.

I nuzzled his neck, as he reached his arms behind him and undid my belt, then awkwardly unzipped my pants. While he did that, I reached around and grabbed him by the cock. He was hard, straining. It was a nice handful, longer than I'd expected. I liked it. My jeans slipped down my hips and my cock popped out. I'd skipped underwear that day. It was somewhere around, I just hadn't felt like digging for it. Besides, it was sexy to go without sometimes. Mickey rubbed my prick up and down the crack of his ass while I pumped his. I chewed on his neck and managed to elicit a nice long moan.

A few minutes later we were crawling onto the makeshift bed I'd created on the floor. Our clothes had come off while traversing the few feet between the window and my temporary bedroom. Mickey was even better looking without his clothes. His belly was tight and his chest wide. He was muscled but not overly. I thought we might roll around for a bit first, but he got on his stomach and lifted his ass in the air. That was my cue.

"I'll be right back," I said and went to get the condom and lube out of the bathroom. Mickey kept his ass in the air and his face in the pillow. "Hurry," he said. I did the best I could, given my unfamiliarity with condoms. I got the package open and rolled it down my cock, then lubed up my swathed dick and his ass. I aimed my cock and pushed into him.

"Oh, fucking Christ," he moaned. I wasn't sure if that was a good thing or not. I pumped him slowly a few times to see if he'd kick me out. When he didn't, I held him by the hips and began to drive into him hard and fast. I ran my hands down his back to his shoulders and grabbed onto them to leverage myself each time I pounded into him.

"I like way your hands feel on me," he whispered.

I tried to comply by running my hands across his wide back, slipping around and tweaking his nipples. Placing my big hands on his narrow waist.

"That's it, just like that. Make me happy," he said. Making him happy seemed like a tall order, but if he meant for the next few minutes I might be able to pull it off.

Aside from the making of dubious choices, drinking has two very common effects on fucking. One is that it can make an erection impossible. Two, is that it can make coming a challenge. Usually you got one or the other. As I was fucking Mickey, I began to realize the second effect was taking hold. Which might have been fine, except I wanted to come. I really wanted to come. I rammed into him as hard as I could. Then I told him to squeeze his ass, tight. I closed my eyes and tried thinking about Joseph, that I was fucking Joseph, that it was Joseph's ass squeezing my dick. It seemed like forever but it was probably just a minute later that I came. I shivered. Gave Mickey's ass a few final pumps and than rolled off him to lie on the bedding. I pulled the condom off and dropped it onto the carpet next to the bedding. I'd deal with it later.

Almost immediately, Mickey was up and looking for his clothes.

"What are you doing?" I asked.

"Fucking gives me energy. I could go for a three mile run."

Sometimes fucking gave me energy, too. But not that much.

I stretched out to pull my coat closer so I could get to my cigarettes. When I did, I rolled into a puddle of Mickey's cum. "Oh, I didn't know you came."

"Of course I came. You think I'd have let you stop if I hadn't?"

"We just met. I don't know what you'd do."

"Okay. For future reference, you're not done unless I come."

"Got it."

He noticed the condom on the floor. He bent over and picked it up daintily between two fingers. "What's this?"

"It's a condom."

"Yeah, I can see that. You just fucked me with a condom?"

"Yes. I did."

"What do you think? I'm gonna get pregnant? It don't work that way."

"The condom prevents disease. You know, AIDS."

"You don't have to worry about that, only fags get AIDS."

I was momentarily stunned. "And what are you and I?"

"We're men. You don't think you're a fag, do you? Come on. Fags are little flitty things who talk with a lisp and like to play with girl's hair. I'm not like that. Neither are you."

I didn't think my lack of a lisp would save me from AIDS. I didn't think it would save Mickey either. He was dressed. I was relieved that he'd be leaving soon. He must have misread my look though, because he said, "I'd stay but I don't sleep on the fucking floor."

"Some other time then," I said.

"Yeah, call me when you get a bed." He pulled a business card out of his pocket and put it on the windowsill. I could have gotten up and given him one of mine but I didn't bother. Less than a minute later he walked out of my apartment.

Chapter Nineteen

I woke up on Sunday morning with a hangover that pulsed and thundered like a Kansas tornado. Not that I'd ever been in a Kansas tornado, but they look pretty bad on the news. A couple of ideas floated around in my head as I took a bath. One was that I needed to get a shower curtain. Another was something that Sugar and Brian were talking about. Drug addicts got AIDS. Why did I think that meant something? Then the word "lesions" popped into my soggy head. *What were lesions exactly?* I wondered. They were blemishes. Sores. Tumors. Ross had lesions on his neck. Red and purple spots. Wes Berkson had lesions on his arm and his ankles. He was a drug addict. Shit. He had Karposi's Sarcoma. He had AIDS. I got out of the bathtub and threw up into the sink. It didn't help the pounding in my head one bit.

I brushed the taste of bile out of my mouth and then put on a lot of Polo. I stank of alcohol and knew it. But there was nothing I could do about it. Looking out the window, the sky was hazy and a little foggy. I tried to think where my umbrella was in case it started to rain and realized I had no idea. I finished dressing and left to go find my car. It was parked about half a block down from

Brian's. He was up in his condo asleep with Franklin. I envied them. I wanted to be asleep.

Driving out to Edison Park, I tried to think what it meant that Wes Berkson had AIDS. That was probably the thing he told his wife that caused her to stab him. Except that she killed Jane Weeks earlier that same day. Did Jane have AIDS too? Was she the one who gave it to Wes? Wes must have told Madeline that he was sick. And that Jane was sick.

So if AIDS was the reason then Madeline already knew. She already knew and planned the whole thing. It wasn't a crime of passion it was the premeditated murder of two people. But why? Why kill people who were going to die anyway?

Then I remembered the insurance. Melody had said buying it was Wes' idea. Not only did she kill a dying man, but his death would have meant—wait, no. Wouldn't he have had to have a medical exam to get that much insurance? Okay, he might have found some kind of policy that didn't require an exam but the minute they suspected he knew he had AIDS when he bought the policy they would cancel payment. The insurance was a dead end. The act of a desperate man and not much more. No, what I wanted to figure out was why? Why did Madeline kill two people dying of AIDS?

I pulled up in front of Mrs. Harker's condo. Really, I just wanted to put my seat back and fall asleep. It was still morning. I could sleep for another hour or two and then go in. Or, I could get this over with, and go home and go back to sleep. I decided on the latter. Mrs. Harker answered my buzz quickly. She opened the door in the midst of putting on her coat. Picking up her purse off a side table, she yelled over her shoulder, "Boy! You come now. Is time."

"Is time for what?" I asked.

"Is time for church."

"Oh," I said, wishing I'd been smart enough to drive around the corner and take that nap. Terry popped up behind Mrs. Harker. He was clean and neatly dressed in a gray suit. I'd never seen it before, so I had to guess that Mrs. Harker had bought it for him.

"Hey," he said to me.

"Hey," I said back. "All right. I'll drive you guys to church."

"No. Not in ugly car."

"Okay, you want to take the bus, go ahead. I'll wait here."

She shook her head at me and said, "Come."

Reluctantly, I walked into the condo, which smelled of baking meat, and then followed her into the galley kitchen. I hadn't thought about it in a long time, but I knew there was a garage just off the kitchen. I think only the first floor condos had them, while the ones on the second floor were shit out of luck. Inside the garage was Harker's 1979 Lincoln Versailles. It was a small four-door sedan built on a Granada's frame and painted a peachy flesh color with the vinyl half roof matching the color perfectly.

"You want me to drive you to church in this?"

Harker had always kept the car up immaculately. Now though, it was dusty and in need of a good polish. It had been sitting there for at least a year and a half. I wasn't even sure it would start. She took a set of keys out of her coat pocket and held them out to me. "Yes, you take to church. Then you keep. Sell ugly car."

"Why does she keep saying your car's ugly? This one's pretty—"

I raised a hand to stop him. The Versailles was an ugly car and it drove like a waterbed. But, it would draw a lot less attention than the Nova. And, I could sell the Nova and split the money with Mrs. Harker. Well, try to split the money with her. She probably wouldn't take it, but she might allow me to reimburse her for whatever she spent on Terry.

My stomach flopped when I opened the door and sat in the driver's seat. It smelled like stale cigarette smoke and cologne laced with cinnamon. It smelled of Harker. Well, it smelled like the inside of a car, but it also smelled of Harker. I wasn't sure I was ready to have something of Harker's, wasn't sure I was ready to remember him fondly. I was mad at him. I'd been mad at him for a long time. Driving his car everywhere meant I'd have to be on better terms with the memory of him. I put the key in the ignition and turned. The engine whined into life. Mrs. Harker and Terry climbed in and I drove to St. Boniface the Martyr.

Before we walked in, I took Terry by the arm and told Mrs. Harker that I was going to have a cigarette before mass. She frowned at me but went into the church. I don't know why she hated my smoking so much. Harker smoked. Not as much as I did, and not much at all after he got sick, but still, he'd smoked. I lit up and gave Terry a stern look.

"How are you and Mrs. Harker getting along?"

218 | Marshall Thornton

"She's a bitch."

That was hard to deny but I felt like I shouldn't let him get away with it anyway. "You should be more respectful at your age."

He shrugged.

"She feeds you. She takes you shopping and buys you shit. She makes sure you do your homework. And she keeps you out of trouble."

His eyes narrowed. "Have you been spying on us?"

"No. I just know what she's like. She's not that bad."

"She calls me 'boy.' I miss Brian."

"You miss Brian's computer game."

"I like Brian."

"He's started dating someone, so maybe you need to give him some space."

"That Franklin asshole?"

"Again, more respect." But again he'd hit the nail on the head. "I think Franklin's going to be around for a while. And if he makes Brian happy, that's cool. Look, I rented an apartment. You can stay with me some of the time." After I get set up and put a lock on the bedroom door."

"How long do I have to stay with Mrs. Harker?"

"Let me talk to Brian. Maybe we'll start with you coming into the city for weekends and see how it goes." That earned me a scowl but nothing worse. I ground out my cigarette on the sidewalk and said, "Come on, we need to go in to mass."

"I'm not even Catholic."

"Then why were your parents sending you to Catholic school?"

"Because they hate me."

I shrugged. "That's why most people send their kids to Catholic school."

Mass was mass. Being Easter there was a bit more pomp and ceremony. The high school choir came in and sang something with a lot of Glorias. The Homily was given by Father Dewes, who was an older priest I'd met and liked a lot. In fact, he'd been instrumental in our overseeing Terry's emancipation. His subject was "The Gift of Christ," in which he talked about what Christ's story meant to all of us. How it embodied the promise of rebirth after struggle. How God offered us rebirth again and again in our lives. I thought he did a good job, though some of the older parishioners looked displeased. As a priest, Father Dewes would never be a good fit for those who preferred fire and brimstone and condemnation. After mass we were able to chat with him for a moment. He seemed pleased with the way Terry looked, even though the kid was quiet to the point of rudeness. As we walked to the car, I asked him, "You don't like Father Dewes?"

"He's all right, I guess."

I was beginning to realize that was high praise from a teenager.

"Is good priest. You respect," Mrs. Harker pronounced. And I nearly cringed having said something similar to Terry twice before mass. I wasn't used to being so in tune with her.

When we got back to the condo, I asked if I could use the phone. I made sure to say that it was for business so

Mrs. Harker didn't have a chance to glower at me. Her phone was in the living room sitting on a special table next to a rocking chair. I went over and dialed Owen's beeper number. After the prompt, I put in Mrs. Harker's phone number.

While most of America was having ham with too much pineapple and brown sugar, we had a roast leg of lamb. "Is tradition," she said as she put it on the table. To my surprise, Terry helped her bring out hard-boiled eggs, sausages, rice, peas with little onions, an amazing loaf of marbled bread, chocolates and fruit.

"Do you need help?" I asked at one point

That earned me a dirty look. "You are guest."

I thought I was more than a guest, I mean, she did just give me a car. But I decided not to argue the point. Before they sat down she told Terry to get me a beer. He brought out two Czechvars, one for me and one for Mrs. Harker. That was something of a surprise. At Brian's he barely lifted a finger. At Brian's he would have tried to have one himself. Something was beginning to dawn on me. She rarely gave me a Czechvar and she rarely drank. When she did it was always some kind of celebration. Sure, it was holiday, but I felt like there was more going on. I'd done something right and Mrs. Harker was thanking me.

The phone rang as we began to fill out plates.

"I'm sure that's for me," I said before Mrs. Harker could get up. "I just beeped someone."

"Beep? What is beep?"

"Terry explain that for me, please. I'll be two minutes."

I walked into the living room and picked up the phone.

"You rang?" Owen Lovejoy, Esquire said.

"Are you going to say that every time?"

"Why not? People say hello every time they pick up the phone, don't they?"

"All right. Yes, I rang. Look, I think I know why Madeline killed her husband."

"You do?"

"Is there any possibility we can see her?"

"You mean today?"

"Are there visiting hours on Sunday?"

"As her attorney I have expanded access, but let me set it up for tomorrow morning."

"Do you…" Even though we'd been fucking on and off for more than a year, I still felt like I was being nosey. "Are you seeing someone?"

"Yes, I am."

That annoyed me a little. People seemed to be pairing up. Like all of Boystown was playing a big game of musical chairs, and all I got was a priest who wouldn't put out and a mobster who didn't think he was gay. That part of my life was definitely not going well.

"Congratulations," I said with as much enthusiasm as I could muster.

"Thanks. Before we do this though, you're going to have to give me a hint. Why do you want to see her?"

222 | Marshall Thornton

"Wes Berkson had AIDS. I think Jane Weeks did, too."

There was silence on the line.

"So Madeline thought they gave it to her and she killed them for it? Is that what you're thinking?" he guessed.

"Something like that. I'd like to hear what she's got to say. Maybe I've got it completely wrong."

"All right. Let me see I can make arrangements. I'll call you back."

Chapter Twenty

I spent another two hours with Mrs. Harker and Terry. Before I left I flipped through her yellow pages and found a place called Mattress World on Touhy near Western. As I drove there in Harker's Lincoln, I wondered if they'd be open. It was Easter, after all, and a lot of stores were closed. But when I pulled up in front, they were open. So then I wondered if they were Jewish. I knew Jews had Passover to deal with, but I think that, like Easter, moved around. In fact, as I was thinking about it, I remembered a priest saying that the last supper took place as part of Passover. So, Easter had to always fall after Passover. Right?

The store was small. I'd expected a larger place, but Mattress World was one narrow storefront between a cleaners and a pizza place, both of which were closed. The signage in the window promised that I wouldn't find better prices anywhere else and that "No One Sells 4 Less." By the time I left the store I figured that other places must have been charging an arm and a leg because I hit my credit card for nearly three hundred dollars. Still, they promised to deliver the mattress on Wednesday morning so I was happy that I only had a few more days of sleeping on the floor.

It would have been nice if they'd sold sheets and bedspreads and pillows, but Mattress World was strictly mattresses. I'd have to go to Marshall Fields or Carson Pirie Scott the next day when I was downtown staking out the Federal Building. In the afternoon I'd take a break and walk over to State Street. Thinking about shopping for new sheets made me feel kind of weird. This wasn't the kind of thing I did on my own. Making a home. It didn't feel like me; but then again, it felt good. It was a new beginning and I'd needed it.

I'd thought that Joseph might be a new beginning, as well. But he wasn't. It hurt a little, but I had to be honest, given the things I'd been through it was barely a scratch. Which led me to the oddest thought. After losing Harker the way I had, after punishing myself for killing the Bughouse Slasher, there weren't many things I wouldn't be able to get through. At least, I hoped that was true.

After picking up a six-pack of Miller and a frozen Celeste pizza at the Jewel, I went home and learned how to use my oven. While it was heating up it emitted a dusty odor that was gone by the time the pizza was finished. I put my Walkman on, turned up the George Benson, sipped my beer, munched my pizza, and watched the light fade away over the lake.

Owen beeped me at eight-thirty the next morning. I was still asleep and had been for a long time. Of course, I didn't have a phone yet, so I had to get dressed, take the elevator down ten stories, and walk around the corner to the Melrose where they had a payphone next to the men's room. When I got Owen on the phone, he told me to meet him in front of Division IV of Cook County Jail in a half an hour. It was tight, but I managed to find my car, drive down to 27th Street and Sacramento, hunt for a parking place—enough of a challenge that I actually prayed to Mother Cabrini—and wait for him in front of the barbed wire gates. He was ten minutes late.

Once he got there, we were able to get past the bureaucracy rather quickly, and before I knew it we were deep inside the red brick building. It was certainly a lot easier than the last time I'd visited someone in the County Jail. A guard led us to a small room with a wooden table and a couple of chairs. It was a nice room, though. Almost as nice as a conference room in an office. Other than the lack of windows and the harsh florescent light above our heads, we could have been anywhere.

After the guard left us, Owen set his briefcase on the table and rolled his eyes. "I must find out who their decorator is. He's done wonders."

"I don't think their goal is to make you want to stay."

"True. She's lucky she's a woman. Conditions on the men's side are so much worse."

We sat. Owen took a legal pad out of his briefcase. We waited.

"Why is Madeline here at all. Wouldn't they grant bail?"

"Bail was set at five hundred thousand dollars. If you use a bondsman they charge ten percent guilty or innocent. Fifty thousand dollars."

I whistled. "She didn't have it?"

"She didn't have that and enough to pay our fee. Our fee on this should run about seventy-five." Seventy-five thousand dollars for a murder defense. Justice was expensive. I hoped I never needed it.

"Her parents couldn't help?"

"They are helping. But there are the kids to consider. When you're in prison they pay you like twenty cents an hour for whatever work you do. Hard to raise kids on that."

We waited. Owen made a few notes on his pad. I grew bored.

"We took Sugar Pilsen to see Sugar Pills the other night."

"The drag queen?"

"Yeah. I think they fell deeply in love."

"So that's why you're a little green around the gills?"

"Still?" I'd thought the holiday dinner Mrs. Harker fed me had straightened me out. Apparently that, and all the sleep I'd gotten, hadn't made much of a dent. Before I could say anything else, the door opened and a guard led Madeline Levine-Berkson into the room. She wore a shapeless gray uniform that looked like medical scrubs. She was thinner than she was in the pictures I'd seen in the newspaper. There she was a little pudgy and scattered looking. Here she was sharp-edged and controlled. Her hair was dark and scraggly, most of the blonde had been cut off.

When the guard shut the door, Owen said, "Hello Madeline, how are you?"

"Better than I should be."

"This is Nick Nowak. He's our investigator. He's been working on your case."

"Which is over."

"He's been helping me look into what people might say if we let them speak for you."

She looked at me suspiciously. "And?"

"After talking to people I have some questions to ask you," I said.

"All right."

"On your husband's autopsy—"

"Wait. You just said you were talking to people. Why are you reading the autopsy?"

"People told me your husband was a drug addict. I wanted to see if the autopsy bore that out. He had lesions on his ankles and his—"

"People should have kept their mouths shut. I don't want any—"

"I understand that Madeline," Owen said. "The thing is. It's beginning to sound as if we could have mounted a much more successful defense."

"You thought your husband gave you AIDS," I said. "Is that why you killed him?"

"I don't want to talk about this."

"Nothing's going to happen that you don't want to happen," Owen said. "But it's better if we at least talk about things."

She seemed to chew her tongue for a moment then said, "I have no idea if he gave me AIDS. I feel fine."

"Madeline, can you tell us why you killed your husband," Owen asked, making his voice sincere and soothing.

"And his girlfriend," I added.

Madeline flashed me a look. Out of the corner of my eye, I think I saw Owen flash me one, too. She took a deep breath and let it out.

"It was the insurance policy. He thought he was doing something good for us. I told him it would backfire, that they'd find out what he died of. I refused to go along with it. Then I found out he'd bought the policies anyway. Forged my signature. I could see what would happen. He was going to die. They'd demand a reason. When they found out, they'd accuse me of fraud and it would all come out. Everyone would know. Even if I got off, no one would go to the dentist whose husband had AIDS. The dentist who might have AIDS. He'd ruined everything."

But why kill him the way she did? I wondered. Why not try to hide it? Why not make it look liked an accident? The questions began to answer themselves. She didn't want his illness to be discovered so she couldn't risk an autopsy without forgone conclusion. The ME needed to see the cause at a glance. Poison would have been too dangerous that way. Hiring someone to kill him had too many risks. Pushing him down the stairs—then it hit me. This had been about the sentencing all along.

"Owen, what's the sentence for first-degree murder?"

"Twenty years to life."

I looked Madeline in the eye and said, "You knew that, didn't you? You made it look like second-degree murder so you'd get a lighter sentence."

"I was always a fan of *Perry Mason*," she said. I decided not to point out that his clients were always innocent.

Sitting back in my chair, I couldn't help but be a little impressed. She'd manipulated the whole thing so that she'd get the minimum sentence. Owen didn't seem as impressed. In fact, he seemed not to notice what had just happened.

"I think the best thing to do is to simply let you make a statement and leave it at that. I'm concerned that someone might mention the drug addiction and then the whole thing begins to unravel. If I'd known all along I could have come up with a better strategy, but at this point…it complicates things." And then he added dryly, "Besides, you seem to know what you're doing."

After I said goodbye to Owen, I drove back to Boystown and found a parking place on Buckingham. Then I walked over to the Melrose again, this time to have breakfast. I was so hungry I was beginning to feel nauseated. I ordered the lumberjack breakfast, which could also have been called the eat-until-you-burst breakfast, a glass of orange juice and a cup of coffee. I had both papers and planned to spend the next hour eating and reading. Then I'd head back to my apartment and dress-up like a priest.

The *Daily Herald* and *The Tribune* both had articles about something we almost, sort of, kind of, already knew. AIDS was caused by a virus. They'd discovered it and named it. They'd found it in a laboratory and called it HTLV-III. Now it was definite. It wasn't just rumors or hints being printed in alternative newspapers; it was mainstream so it was real. And more than that, I guess. It wasn't just some virus, it was now a specific identifiable virus. And if it was something they could indentify, then it might be something they could cure. As I ate my breakfast, I tried not to be too optimistic. It wasn't something I could contribute to. I wasn't a scientist. I was just a guy who figured things out. I needed to put the news aside and focus on what I was doing. But it wasn't easy.

Hope was every bit as contagious as the virus.

By eleven o'clock I was back on the Federal Plaza begging money and staring people up and down. I positioned myself on a different corner than I'd worked on Friday, and settled in for a long afternoon. I still didn't expect to find Prince Charles this way, but…well just but. I watched as people walked by in all sizes and shapes, all colors, all kinds of beliefs reflected in their dress, some with crosses, some with T-shirts that proclaimed an affinity for Led Zeplin or Ronald Reagan or *The A-Team*. Blue suits with red ties were practically popular.

My feet were killing me after an hour. The sidewalk and plaza were made out of some kind of crushed granite that had been mixed with concrete. It was hard to stand on for a long time. I wondered if there was someplace nearby that I could go for a pair of insoles or arch supports. The money flowed in faster than it had on the Friday before. Of course, Friday had been Good Friday, and even though it's not a Federal holiday it was a day that a lot of people took off. Now they're back and primed to donate by an Easter sermon.

What was I going to do if I saw someone suspicious? I wondered. I should have a plan. I couldn't exactly throw aside a bucket full of change and run after them. I mean, a priest chasing down a mobster type in the middle of the Loop was almost laughable. I could casually follow someone, but then there was the bucket. No, all I'd be able to do would be observe, make mental notes about appearance and then talk to Jimmy, I suppose. After my phone call with Connors, I doubted he'd let me come down and look at any of the books they had full of known Outfit members. For the second time, I thought I might need one of those super tiny cameras they used in spy movies. Well, I needed one twice a year and that made it hard to justify the cost. That, and the fact that I giggled at the idea of someone chasing after me for the microfilm.

Around two, I decided to take a break and go over to the French Bakery to see if Brian was there. I was still full from breakfast, but I might just have a cup of soup or something light. The lunch rush was well over by the time I walked up the steps to the restaurant on the second floor of the storefront on Madison and Dearborn, passing the real French bakers they had behind a window making croissants for the next morning. People knew me there, so no one bothered to stop me as I walked through the restaurant to the extra dining room in the back where the waiters had lunch after their shift. Brian sat at a small table with the bartender I liked, Lu. Lu had red hair cut into a punk mullet, a few chunks artfully cut out of her ears and a voice like back alley gravel. After we said hello, I asked Brian, "Did you see the paper?"

"The virus?" he asked.

"Yeah, they found it."

"I know. I talked to Sugar before I came in; she'd already been on the phone for two hours. She talked to a couple of doctors. They don't think we should get too excited."

"Why not?" Lu asked. "It's seems like great news."

"It's a virus. No one's ever cured a virus."

"What about the flu?" I asked. "There's a vaccine for the flu."

"It takes years to develop a vaccine. Sometimes a decade. And it's not a cure. It's a prevention."

So we were shit out of luck. This news didn't help Ross. It didn't help a lot of people. Possibly not Brian. Possibly not me.

As though he'd read my thoughts, Brian said, "I tried calling Ross this morning. They wouldn't let me talk to him. They said he was getting better. That if he talked to me he might relapse."

"That sucks," Lu said. "I don't know why he had to go down there. We would have taken care of him."

"They promised to save him. It's hard not to believe that when it's all you've got."

Chapter Twenty-One

The afternoon was deadly dull and I let my mind wander. I imagined myself as Charles Bronson swooping down on Normal, Illinois, and dragging Ross out of his parents' trailer to bring him back where he belonged. I knew I wouldn't do any such thing, but it felt good to fantasize about. I wondered what Harker would think of my apartment? Would he like it? Or would he miss living in the basement? I knew he'd hate what I was doing for Jimmy. He'd be afraid I was becoming the Outfit's guy. And maybe I was. But I didn't think Jimmy had killed the Perellis, so the task force shouldn't just get to pin it on him. Maybe if I thought he killed them I'd be a little more squeamish about the whole thing.

Around five forty-five, foot traffic was thinning out and I noticed a middle-aged man come up out of the subway. He had a heavy beard, wore a rumpled leisure jacket in gray, a blue polo shirt, and polyester plaid paints to match the shirt and jacket. He had an unlit cigar in his mouth. My heart sped up when I saw him. Maybe this was going to work. I watched as he headed toward the lobby entrance on the Dearborn side of the building. I hurried to the entrance near me, clutching my plastic bucket of change to my chest. I was closer to the elevators; he had to walk across the spacious lobby. I hurried around and stood on the side of the elevators he was heading toward and stood there with my bucket out. If I could get him to drop some change in, I'd also get a damn good look at him.

I stood there nervously. An older woman with a pill box hat and half veil stood in front of me like a time traveler from the sixties. She opened her white patent leather purse and began a search for change. I wanted to yell at her to hurry-the-fuck-up, but couldn't break character. I was a priest, after all. She was still poking around when the guy walked by me without a glance. I tried to memorize his face. Heavy brow, eyes so brown they were almost black, a nose that looked like it had been broken a half dozen times. Just as the woman finally plunked some money into my bucket, he was at the elevator, stepping in a car, disappearing. I wished for a moment that we were in one of the older buildings that told you what floor the car was on. I could watch the numbers change until the car stopped. Newer buildings like this didn't work that way. I had no idea what floor he was going to.

Briefly, I considered jumping into an elevator and going to the twenty-third floor. I wouldn't get there in time. If he were going there he would beat me to it and be safely tucked behind the office door of the task force. I'd have no idea if he was in there or not. I decided the smart thing to do was to go and stand by the subway entrance. Sooner or later he'd come out and then I could follow him home. I stood there wondering who the guy was. He was a good thirty-five years younger than Jimmy. Was he someone Jimmy had mentored? Was he on Jimmy's crew?

How long would he be in there? If he was Prince Charles he could be in there for hours being questioned.

I was busy trying to think how long I might be standing there, when a gray Ford LTD pulled up to the curb. It was a boxy sedan. The kind favored by Federal agencies. The doors opened and three people got out. One of the Federal agents I'd been in the elevator with and two other people I recognized. Two people who knew Jimmy. The guy I'd just picked out and was trying to figure out how to tail was nobody. Prince Charles was standing in front of me. But I couldn't be sure he was a prince at all, or rather which of them was the prince. One of the people with the agent was Jimmy's granddaughter, Deanna Hansen. The other was her boyfriend and low-level Outfit scum, Turi Bova.

I'd run across Deanna once before. I was looking for whoever blew up my Plymouth Duster, and for a while I suspected Turi Bova of having done it. That was how I learned that Deanna was involved with the much older mobster. It didn't take much to figure out Jimmy wouldn't like it. It also didn't take much to realize I'd be a fool to keep that information to myself, so I forced Deanna to confess her sins to her grandfather. I'd thought that had ended their association, but I was wrong.

Deanna hadn't forgotten me either. Her eyes flared when she saw me. She nudged her boyfriend and Turi looked over at me. Sheer hatred turned his face beet red. It was comforting that there was a Federal agent right there, since it prevented anyone from pulling a gun. Calmly, I walked down into the subway.

Of course, I wasn't calm. Not even close. I now knew something that I had to tell people. I had to tell Owen and then somebody had to tell Jimmy. I was tempted to tell

Owen and then let him deal with Jimmy, but, given that I actually had something to do with this, given that his granddaughter might have had no reason to seek revenge on Jimmy if I hadn't forced her...yeah, I was sort of, maybe, responsible. I needed to tell him myself.

After I got off at the Belmont stop, I hurried home and quickly changed my clothes. Then I walked around the neighborhood looking for my car. At first I was looking for the Nova, then I remembered I actually had the Versailles and the Nova was now sitting out in Edison Park with a makeshift for sale sign in the window. Remembering which car I was looking for made it a lot easier. I found it on Melrose and drove out to Oak Park.

I tried to work out what I'd seen and what it meant. Who was Prince Charles? Turi or Deanna? As far as I knew, Turi didn't have anything to do with Jimmy. He wasn't high enough up in the Outfit to know Jimmy's business. And I couldn't imagine Jimmy giving him the time of day. That left Deanna. Of course it was Deanna. If Turi was the informant he would have made her stay home. A macho guy like Turi would never let her come along for support. And a macho guy like Turi wouldn't let her come alone if she was the informant. Deanna was Prince Charles. They'd called her that to throw us of the scent. It had worked.

But that raised an important question. *How did she know so much about her grandfather's activities?*

Jimmy opened the door himself. He wore a white shirt, black slacks and a pair of plaid flannel slippers. His hair was a bit disheveled as though I'd just woken him from a nap. Since it was after dinnertime, I assumed he'd let the maid go for the day. I apologized for showing up so late, though it was only about seven and the sun wouldn't fully set for another hour.

"It's important, Jimmy," I assured him.

He led me into a parlor just off the foyer. I'd never been in there before. The room was decorated to look as though it was a British drawing room. Or rather, the American idea of a British drawing room gleaned mostly from movies. There were antique tables with vases against the walls, an unused fireplace, an Oriental rug laid over wall to wall carpet, a comfortable sofa in a floral print, and carved wooden chairs with wide upholstered seats which were probably named after some French king. Jimmy sat on the sofa while I sat on one of the chairs.

"The informant is your granddaughter, Deanna," I said as simply and directly as I could. Jimmy pushed himself back into the sofa; he looked as though he'd just been hit by a gust of air.

"You're sure?"

"I saw them get out of a car with a Federal agent on their way into the Federal Building where Operation Tea and Crumpets is housed."

We were quiet for quite a long time. Softly, he said the girl's name once, except he pronounced it Dina or Dean-a. Which I supposed was the Italian way. A gold clock in a glass bubble sat on the mantel. I listened to it tick off the seconds.

"The diary is real, isn't it Jimmy?" That was the only way Deanna would know anything about her grandfather's activities unless—

"Yes. I kept a diary," he admitted.

"Why did you lie to me about that?"

"It's a very dangerous book. I can't have people knowing it exists. You can't ask people about it, do you understand?"

"I won't say anything to anyone. But your lawyer should know."

He shrugged.

"You still have the diary, don't you? Deanna just made a copy, right?"

"No. She stole it."

"You've known that all along."

"I knew it was gone. I didn't know my granddaughter took it."

"Who did you think took it?"

"My driver. The maid. I got rid of them."

"You fired them?" I asked hopefully.

He looked a little offended. "I wouldn't do more than that without proof."

"According to the files, Prince Charles–Deanna–has told them, repeated conversations the two of you have had. Is that true?"

"Cautionary tales meant to put the girl on the right track."

"Have you seen her recently?"

He shook his head. "She wants to come next week."

"She'll be wearing a wire. Or at least she would have been. They saw me, too."

"She won't come then."

I thought about the situation for a moment. I had to think of something constructive to suggest. "If they indict you, the Feds will have to provide your defense with a copy of the diary. But they're going to do their best to stall. You need to try to remember everything you can about what you put in that diary. My guess is that your lawyers will want to find inconsistencies, things that aren't true. If they can cast doubt on some of what's in the diary then all of it becomes suspect."

"Why would I write things that aren't true?"

"Jimmy, you'll never admit that you wrote it. If we find anything in there that doesn't fit, then we'll be able to say that you didn't write it."

He thought for a moment, then nodded.

Not sure I wanted the answer, I asked, "Does this mean you did order the death of the Perellis?"

He just looked at me. It was a look that made me a queasy. But what did I expect, really? That Jimmy was secretly a Girl Scout?

"Getting Nino Jr. to say his father confessed would be close to the truth?"

"No. It wouldn't be. The Nose didn't do the job."

I was afraid to ask who did. Somehow this would all be worse if Jimmy killed them himself. It didn't matter though. Operation Tea and Crumpets was wrong. They were just making things up and pushing people around until they agreed. Wasn't that every bit as wrong as what Jimmy had done? If they got away with doing something like this to Jimmy, then what would they do to innocent people? I was rationalizing and knew it. But it did make me feel better for a moment. But only for a moment.

"What does it say in your diary about the Perellis?"

"That N took care of the Ps."

"Who is N?" If it wasn't Jimmy, I could ask.

He shook his head. I decided not to press him. A minute later he said, "I don't believe she did this to me."

"The people we love can do terrible things."

He looked at me as though he'd made it to his eighties without ever suspecting this.

Driving home, I turned it all over in my head. The pieces fit. I wasn't sure if they fit because they belonged together or because they'd been stubbornly jammed together like pieces of a puzzle with too much sky. But I couldn't think of any reason for Jimmy to lie to me. He was very likely going to prison, sent there by his own granddaughter. I put the whole thing out of my head and drove. I'd done my job. I'd found the informant, and I could relax. I didn't think Jimmy would try to "persuade" his own grandchild. The girl was safe and the best that could be hoped for was that Cooke, Babcock, and Lackerby would find a technicality to get him off. And, hopefully, I'd keep getting paid to make that happen.

The sun had just set and I was nearly home when my beeper went off. I looked at the number and didn't recognize it. I was close to the Walgreen's, so I stopped at the pay phone they had outside near the entrance. I plunked my quarter in and dialed the number. After one ring a man answered. He didn't bother with hello or any other niceties.

"Nowak. You didn't quit your job like you were supposed to."

"No. I have this weird addiction to paying my rent."

"If you know what's good for you, you'll quit the job." And I'd just been hoping it would continue for a long time.

"Your name's Devlin and you're harassing me. If you don't stop I'll report you to the State's Attorney."

That cracked him up. He was still laughing when he hung up. I stood there for a moment with the phone still to my ear. He was probably right. The idea that the State's Attorney would take any action against someone working on Operation Tea and Crumpets was a joke. I had to do something, though. I had to take some action to keep Devlin from making good on his threats. I hung up the phone and reversed my course.

A few minutes later I was in my office. I opened up the bottom drawer of my desk and pulled out my Sig Sauer. For years I'd worn it everywhere I went. Hell, I wore it fucking a few times. But then after I killed Joseph Gorshuk I stopped feeling that the danger was outside of me. Most of the time, I was the most dangerous thing in the room, and I knew it. Carrying a gun only made that feeling worse, so I stopped. I slipped the gun into my pocket and left the office.

I headed back to Belmont and walked toward the lake, walked under the Drive, and headed toward the Rocks. The Rocks are a seawall made of enormous terraced stone blocks that are now covered in sometimes-clever graffiti. In the summer it's the place where gay boys put on Speedos to sun themselves and flirt. That night it was dark and the lake seemed restless, rising in waves to beat against the giant stones. I jumped down the rocks to the lowest terrace, took the Sig Sauer out of my pocket, and with as much strength as I could muster threw it out into the lake. I wish I could say it was the first time Lake Michigan had claimed a gun from me, but it wasn't. There was a nice Smith & Wesson Model 28 that had once belonged to me floating around somewhere near Foster. So now Lake Michigan held two of my secrets. I wondered how many other guns were floating around the bottom of the lake. I wondered how many thousands of secrets the lake hid.

I tried to decide whether I should call Connors and tell him I'd been threatened again. I wasn't sure that was necessary and actually thought it might be better if I stayed as far away from him as I could. He'd tampered with evidence and I didn't think there was any way he'd admit to it. Since the evidence was no longer in my possession the most logical thing to assume was that it was lost in the property section. Somewhere there was a record of Connors submitting a search on the gun's ownership. If that came to light, it wasn't good for either of us, but it wasn't terrible. I could say I lost the gun before Gorshuk's death. The fact that the gun ended up in the same cemetery where the man who killed my lover died is just one of those amazing coincidences that happen. As was the fact that Connor's requested an ownership search on a gun that belonged to his partner's lover. But that's all that anyone would ever have. A couple of amazing coincidences. No one could place me in the cemetery. Gorshuk had not been shot so there was no bullet to connect to my gun. In fact, I could argue that if I was in the cemetery with Gorshuk why *didn't* I shoot him? I could argue that it might have been Groshuk who *stole* my gun in an attempt to incriminate me. An attempt that went wrong. My trail of logic made me feel a bit better. I was safe as long as Devlin didn't begin to fabricate evidence. If I didn't know they were completely capable of that, I'd have felt great.

The next morning as I walked over to my office, I stopped at the Walgreen's payphone and called Devlin's number. I didn't want to talk to him, but I did want to find out how the phone was answered. Did they say, "Operation Tea and Crumpets?" Or had they made up some faux company name like "Acme International?" The call was picked up almost immediately and a recorded voice said, "The number you have reached is not in service. Please check the number and try again."

That was creepy.

Chapter Twenty-Two

Life went on. My bed was delivered. I rented a truck, and Brian and Franklin helped me move my big stuff over from my office. I shoved it all in the middle of my place, covered it with some old sheets and painted the walls a slightly darker gray than my apartment on Roscoe had been. The phone company came and installed a telephone. I chose the beige desk model. They didn't come in gray.

Ronald Reagan went to China so that he could look like a diplomat and help his chances for re-election. Most everyone thinks he will get re-elected because America hates details and loves photo opportunities. *Thriller* was replaced as the number one album by *Footloose*, a movie soundtrack. I didn't bother seeing the movie. A town where they banned dancing seemed too ridiculous even for Middle America. Of course, for all I knew it was based on a true story.

Madeline Levine-Berkson spoke in her own defense at her sentencing. She was the only one who spoke. The jury gave her the minimum sentence of four years probation, which is sort of like saying, "Hey, as long as you don't kill anymore husbands everything will be fine." The judge, though, didn't buy it and gave everyone in the courtroom a stern lecture, but apparently that was all he could do.

Giovanni Agnotti AKA Jimmy English was indicted on Monday, April 30, on dozens of counts, including conspiracy and murder. He posted a very pricey bond and surrendered his passport. The trial was unlikely to happen for at least a few months, maybe six, maybe more, which meant that I had a very unfortunate kind of job security. The testimony of Deanna Hansen and the diary were not enough on their own to indict him. The final nail in his coffin was the Nose, Jr. Apparently they'd put enough pressure on him to get him to say what they wanted. He was going to testify that his father confessed on his deathbed to killing the Perellis at Jimmy's behest. I didn't know why he didn't call Cooke, Babcock and Lackerby to get him out of it. Unless, of course, he was the kind of CPA who wasn't really on the up and up and they had something on him.

Terry began coming into town for weekends. Surprisingly, he stopped begging to come back full time. He'd usually come in on Friday night and either stay with Brian in his old room or with me on the pullout. I'd drive him back out to Edison Park for Sunday super. A few weeks after Easter, Mrs. Harker came out into the hallway while I was leaving. I'd managed to sell the Nova and had brought her half the money, money which she refused until I told her to spend it on Terry. My first thought was that she was going to try and give it back again. I was a bit taken back when she asked, "Is boy sick?"

I knew right away what she was asking me. She wasn't wondering if he had a cold. "I don't think so. He's not very experienced."

She thought that over.

"He doesn't seem sick, does he?" I asked.

"No." I was about to leave when she added, "Is terrible thing. AIDS."

"Yes, it is."

She and I knew that all too well.

It took me three weeks to call Joseph. I still had his priestly get up and needed to give it back to him. I really just wanted to find out where he was so I could drive by, drop a bag with his things on his front stoop and speed off. He said he wanted to see me so he could explain himself. I didn't have much patience for that, but I didn't know how to say no.

I suggested we meet at the Glory Hole just to be obnoxious, though The Closet would have been more insulting, I suppose. Instead he asked if he could simply come over.

"Did you paint your apartment like you said you wanted to?" he asked.

"Yeah, I did."

"I'd like to see it."

We agreed that he'd come by the next day. I spent a lot of time in that twenty-some hours looking at my place and adjusting where things were and how they looked. I really had no idea what I was doing, but I did it anyway. My mind made the ridiculous connection that the nicer my place looked the more Joseph would regret going back to the priesthood. And I wanted him to regret it. I wanted him to regret it a lot.

Harker's couch, I couldn't think of it any other way, was a very light beige and looked good with the brown rug and the gray walls. Brian suggested I angle it away from the wall so that there was a nice view when you sat on it. He was right. The director's chairs that Daniel and I had bought together had new canvas in burnt orange and sat across from Harker's couch. I'd gone to The Great Ace and stood there for twenty minutes deciding between green and blue and orange. Actually, I still eyed the chairs suspiciously and wondered if I should go back and get the green canvas. I did get one of their curly-cue extension cords in kelly green. It snaked across the floor behind the grey metal shelves I had which held my TV and VCR on one side, and my turntable and receiver on the other. My Bose speakers sat on the floor on either side of the shelves. My kitchen table sat in front of the wide window, and I enjoyed sitting there in the mornings with a cup of coffee and the *Daily Herald* that showed up at my door every morning. In the evenings, I enjoyed a scotch and worked my way through *Dancer From the Dance*, which I'd picked up at Unabridged Books.

The intercom buzzed exactly five minutes before Joseph was due to arrive. I didn't bother saying hello, I just pressed the button to release the locked door. I was nervous, though I had no reason to be. I wished I'd opened the bottle of wine that I'd bought. He wanted to explain himself, that didn't mean I needed to be sober. I took the bottle of Chardonnay out of the refrigerator and managed to get it uncorked before Joseph knocked.

I opened the door but tried not to look at him. "I'm having a glass of wine, do you want one?" I asked walking back to my tiny little kitchen.

"Sure," he said dubiously.

I set the brand new wine glasses Brian had bought me as a housewarming gift onto the table and filled them.

When I offered one to Joseph, I caught his eye. What I saw there surprised me enough to ask, "So what's going on?"

"I'm leaving."

"You just got here."

"I'm leaving the priesthood."

"Oh. Again?"

"I'm sorry if I've been a little hard to follow."

He put his wine onto the table, then took mine from me and set it next to his. Taking a step forward, he kissed me gently. I kissed him back, my tongue exploring, touching his broken tooth, his tongue, his lips. I pulled him close. Kissed his neck, then whispered into his ear, "You didn't say if you liked what I've done with the place."

"If you bought a bed I'd said what you've done is amazing."

I led him into the bedroom. There wasn't much in there other than the brand new queen-sized bed, a couple of orange crates I used as nightstands, and my old beat up dresser. The bed did have new maroon sheets, a bedspread in a red and brown pattern, and extra fluffy pillows. I didn't have any drapes for the window.

Joseph kicked off his loafers and climbed onto the bed. Already barefoot, I crawled onto the bed to join him. I kissed him some more, pressing my body into his. I could feel his erection rubbing against mine through his pants. I reached down and grabbed hold of it. He moaned like he might pass out. I stopped kissing him and undid his belt, unzipped his jeans and pulled his pants down around his hips. I cupped his balls, pulled his cock away from his belly and slipped the tip into my mouth.

Given that I was fairly certain this was his very first blow job, I applied just about every technique I could think of. I ran my tongue around the glans, I took his dick as deep into my throat as I could, I kept a hand around the base and moved it in rhythm with my mouth, I rubbed the stubble on my chin against him. I pulled out all the stops. And from the panting and occasional oh-my-God-ing he did I was pretty sure I was doing a good job. I had his cock deep in my throat when I realized he was coming. There wasn't much to do but go ahead and swallow.

I tried to remember what it said in the brochure Brian had given me. I wasn't sure this was a good idea, but if it was a virus it seemed entirely possible…but then maybe I was being kind of stupid. Joseph was a virgin. It was fine. I relaxed and ran my tongue over the cum-covered head and felt him shiver.

I sat back and smiled at him. His button-down shirt was still on, his jeans were around his knees, I told him to "Get naked," and we both quickly pulled off our clothes. It was still early enough that some light came through the window. I didn't want to turn on the overhead light. That would feel like we were fucking in an operating theater. I needed to buy a lamp. Or maybe not. In the dim light he seemed to shimmer on the dark sheets. His freckles were scattered all over his chest and shoulders. His belly and hips were ghostly white and then freckles began again on his legs. I start to kiss and lick him around his shoulders. He smelled sweet, faintly like warm bread. I kissed him around his chest. He lay back and let me do what I wanted. I explored his body like it was it was island I wanted to inhabit.

When I got down to his waist, his cock lay flaccid on his hip, sticky, spent. I flipped him over. His ass was unblemished, startling white and plumply square. I kissed each cheek and then slid my tongue down the crack. When I hit his pucker hole he whispered the word "Jesus." I thought I might have to talk to him about that. A former priest really needed to say something else in bed.

I teased his ass until he was breathless, then I reached beneath him and found he was getting hard again. I reached over to the crate on the closet side of the bed and opened a small Indonesian box I'd put there, and filled with condoms and KY.

"What are you doing?" Joseph asked.

"I want to fuck you."

"I don't know…"

"We'll stop if you don't like it. The condom is supposed to make it safer."

"Okay." There was still a bit of concern on his face, but I decided to pull out all the stops just as I had with the blow job, hoping to get the same result. I slipped on the condom and lubed it. After putting more lube on my fingers, I rubbed them around his hole. Then I carefully slid a finger in. "If it feels uncomfortable press down a little." I kept my eyes on his ass and felt around for his prostate. I found the circular button already beginning to harden. Pressing it, rubbing it, I worked it until I saw surprise on Joseph's face. His cock was good and hard so I slipped in another finger. He closed his eyes and sighed heavily.

I whispered, "Relax." I could feel him let go a little, then a little more as I worked his prostate.

"This feels so…different," he said. It didn't seem a good time to ask what it seemed different from, but my guess was masturbation since that was his only real sexual history.

"Just go with it."

I pulled my fingers out of him, positioned myself between his legs and aimed my cock. Then I pushed, slowly but steadily, into him. He let out a ragged gasp. I told him to "Relax" again and went all the way in. I held myself there to give him time to adjust. He whimpered a little and the looked up at me with a questioning look on his face that seemed to say, "Are we really doing this? Does this really feel this good?"

Moving slowly in and out of him, I was carefully not to be as aggressive as I might have been if he were more experienced. I had a leg in each hand and pushed them up into his chest. His face looked as though he was becoming emotional, his eyes glistened with tears. I wondered if he might begin to cry.

Abruptly, he said, "I'm sorry. That's all I can do right now."

"All right," I said, easing out of him. "That's fine. You did really good for a first time."

"It was good, I just…it's a lot."

"I know."

I stayed where I was, slipped the condom off and applied some more KY to both of us. I began jerking us off, a prick in each hand. I wasn't too far off from coming. I kept my eyes locked to his, watching his every reaction, listening to his breath quicken, I knew the minute he came again I'd go with him. I was anxious for him to come, willing him to. And then, cum flew out of him landing just below his collarbone leaving a trail across him like a creamy comet. I popped almost immediately, adding to the mess on his belly.

I hung my head over his and kissed him, still hungry to be close to him. Then I got up and grabbed some tissues from a box on my dresser. After I cleaned us up, I got into bed beside him and pulled him close. He rested his head on my chest. I felt content and comfortable. A lot of things were going my way.

"I don't know how to do this," Joseph whispered into my chest.

"No one does. But we do it anyway."

ALSO BY MARSHALL THORNTON

Desert Run

Full Release

The Perils of Praline, or the Amorous Adventures of a Southern Gentleman in Hollywood

The Ghost Slept Over

My Favorite Uncle

IN THE BOYSTOWN MYSTERIES SERIES

Boystown: Three Nick Nowak Mysteries

Boystown 2: Three More Nick Nowak Mysteries

Boystown 3: Two Nick Nowak Novellas

Boystown 4: A Time For Secrets

Boystown 5: Murder Book

Boystown 6: From The Ashes

Boystown 7: Bloodlines

Marshall Thornton is a novelist, playwright and screenwriter living in Long Beach, California. He is best known for the *Boystown* detective series, which has been short-listed in the Rainbow Awards three times and has also been a finalist for the Lambda Book Award - Gay Mystery three times. Other novels include the erotic comedy *The Perils of Praline, or the Amorous Adventures of a Southern Gentleman in Hollywood*; *Full Release; The Ghost Slept Over* and *My Favorite Uncle*. Marshall has an MFA in screenwriting from UCLA, where he received the Carl David Memorial Fellowship and was recognized in the Samuel Goldwyn Writing awards. He has also had plays produced in Chicago and LA, and stories published in *The James White Review* and *Frontier Magazine*.

21312076R00158

Made in the USA
Middletown, DE
25 June 2015